Rescued by Qaiyaan

A Steamy Sci-Fi Romance

Tamsin Ley

Twin Leaf Press

Paperback version
ISBN-13: 978-1983585838
ISBN-10: 1983585831

Acknowledgments

To my Elite Review Crew, who cheered me on every step of the way. You're the reason I write. And to my fabulous Jitters Critters. I know sheathing a sword will never be the same. Thank you.

Chapter One

"I recognize your ship, Captain Qaiyaan." The voice coming over the ship's comm deepened with menace. "You're interfering with a legal salvage operation."

The two ships rotating helplessly outside Qaiyaan's port screen told a different story than the human on the comm was telling; an eyeful of stars peeked through the blackened hole piercing the Syndicorp passenger ship's hull, while the second, unmarked vessel's short-range lasers glowed from recent use. "Seems you ought to be a bit more generous," Qaiyaan drawled. "What with needing our help and all. I'm gonna take first crack at the salvage, then we'll get you your part. You can have whatever we leave behind."

"I warn you, don't touch that ship!" blustered the voice on the other end.

Normally Qaiyaan'd wish the other pirate captain well and move on. Not today. His crew hadn't had a profitable job in half a Denaidan year. This opportunity was too good to pass up. Besides, anyone who blew a hole in an unarmed passenger transport—Syndicorp or otherwise—left a sour taste in Qaiyaan's mouth. "I could simply wait here. My first mate estimated in half a day we'll have two ships in need of salvage. This is an awful deep part of space to find yourselves without a spare flux modulator."

"You fucking son-of-a-rakwiji-whore bastard! I have powerful friends, and I can make sure you never find safe harbor in this sector again!"

Qaiyaan crossed his arms and glared at the comm. "I'm the *only* friend you have in the galaxy at this moment, so I suggest you be polite."

Noatak, Qaiyaan's first mate, grinned at him from the navigator's seat, the copper sheen of his skin reflecting the multi-colored light from the control panels. The small cockpit, designed for humans, was barely big enough for the two Denaidan males to breathe at the same time. "Want me to take us in for soft docking?"

Qaiyaan watched the human pirate ship complete another slow, helpless turn in the port monitor. "Take us in, but keep an eye out for anything suspicious. Could be a Syndicorp trap."

"Pretty elaborate for a setup." Noatak shook his head, the metal beads decorating his long hair and beard clicking softly.

"Chances of blowing both in-line flux modulators at once *and* not having a spare? Either he's stupid, or it's a setup."

"I say he's stupid." Noatak adjusted the controls to nose the *Hardship* toward the passenger wreckage.

Qaiyaan rose from the captain's chair. Shit happened, especially to ships running less-than-legal activities. He ought to know, having just forked out the proceeds from their latest heist to retrofit a new hull onto the *Hardship's* battle-damaged frame. The black market repairman'd all but asked Qaiyaan to bend over and spread his cheeks. Rotten, cheating bastard.

Turning to the door, he paused and looked over his shoulder at Noatak. "Just be careful. Even if it's not a trap, Syndicorp'll be looking for their missing ship, and I don't want to be caught with our dicks out."

After sealing the control room door, he slid down the ladder to the cargo bay, booted feet clanging against the catwalk grating as he landed. "Mekoryuk! Tovik! All hands on deck!"

Mekoryuk poked his clean-shaven face out of the med bay. He was the only crew member who chose not to wear the customary full beard the Denaida prided themselves on, citing a doctor's need for cleanliness or some such *anaq.* "What is it?"

"Salvage mission. Assume zero atmo. No time for suits. Syndicorp could be riding our ass any minute. Where's Tovik?"

"Where else?" Mek tilted his head toward the end of the hall.

Qaiyaan left the doctor and strode to where the hatch to the engine room stood open. As captain, he could appreciate the well-oiled hum of a ship's engines, but Tovik was a bit too much in love with moving parts. Squatting next to the hole, Qaiyaan yelled, "Tovik! On deck ready for void! And bring a spare in-line flux modulator! Now!"

Knowing his crewmen would comply without further prodding, he headed for the airlock. Through the portal, he watched Noatak guide the magnetic grappler into place. The captain of the human ship was probably apoplectic, watching his cash cow get raped by another ship. *Tough luck.* Qaiyaan'd be sure to leave the replacement flux modulator within reach, but not until the *Hardship* was ready to hightail it out of there.

The first mate finessed the grappler toward the other ship's open airlock, his voice crackling over the internal comm to the cargo bay. "You sure you don't want to take time to suit up?"

Mekoryuk arrived with a med-kit over his shoulder, and Qaiyaan shot him a grin as he answered. "No suits. These *qumli* need the practice."

Tovik pounded up, feet bare as usual, his scruffy beard and hair not quite the full mane of a mature Denaida male. Qaiyaan scowled at him, looking pointedly at his gleaming copper feet. The youngster said he had better control of his ionic abilities if his skin was bare, but one of these days he was going to lose a toe, or worse. At least the boy carried the spare flux modulator, as requested.

While Noatak secured the flexi-tube between the ships, Qaiyaan filled in the other crew members. "I'm not sure what we'll find over there, but it's not likely to be pretty. Grab everything not nailed down. We'll sort our inventories later."

Mek asked, "What about survivors?"

"There's no life signs aboard." Qaiyaan pointed to the modulator in Tovik's hands. "That'll stay with the human ship once we leave. Can you give it a slow push their direction? I don't want it to reach them until we're long gone."

"You bet, Captain!" the young man nodded, likely already calculating trajectory and speed at which to push the thing.

"Stand fast for void!" Noatak's voice echoed through the cargo bay.

Qaiyaan barely had time to summon his ionic shell before the doors cracked open. A blast of air swept past, rattling the flexi-tube as it sucked into the other ship and out the gaping hole in its hull. The Denaidan's ability to withstand vacuum had made them one of the most sought-after races for Syndicorp marine troopers before the catastrophe had ended their world. Now...

Now they were just pirates.

Concentrating on keeping his feet on the deck, Qaiyaan tapped his temple to activate his cochlear implant. A vestige of his days as a trooper, it came in handy in zero atmo when they couldn't bother with suits and the attached comms.

The three crewmen pushed themselves along the flexi-tube into the darkness of the other ship. Tovik, ever prepared, pulled a floodlight from his belt and slapped it to the inner wall of the passenger ship. The illumination exposed a passenger cabin surprisingly gutted of anything passenger-related. No nav-grav seats for humanoids, no methane tanks for garan'uks, not even any acceleration webbing for yanipa-nimayu. Instead, cargo containers of all shapes and sizes floated freely within the cabin, some cracked open and spilling their contents in haloes around them.

What the hell is this ship? Qaiyaan wondered. He'd been expecting the gruesome sight of space-bloated passengers. Not that he minded this alternative. He reached out and grabbed a floating package of hypodermic needles. *Medical supplies?*

He exchanged a glance with Tovik, who shrugged. Whatever this stuff was didn't matter; he'd much rather deal with salable goods than corpses.

Qaiyaan pushed toward the nearest container until he could get a hand on it and shoved the man-sized box toward the flexi-tube, relying on inertia to carry it most of the way. One after another, he moved containers, working until sweat coated his skin beneath his ionic shielding. Even in zero-G, it took effort to hold himself steady and force the heavy boxes into motion. At least twenty minutes passed before he grew light-headed. Using the ionic shell was much like a diver holding his breath, and he knew they'd soon have to come up for air. A tinny voice in his implant did the job for him. "We have incoming on long-range, Captain. Can't yet tell if it's Syndicorp, but they'll be in range for ID in eight minutes."

Anaq. They'd come looking faster than he'd expected. He raised his arm and caught the other men's attention, circling two index fingers overhead to tell them to wrap it up. The men dropped what they were doing and moved toward the exit.

As soon as the door sealed, blessed oxygen began to fill the bay, but it would be a few minutes before there was enough pressure to breathe. Still light-headed, Qaiyaan began helping secure the containers against the floor's mag-locks. He estimated they'd emptied at least half the salvage and was feeling quite pleased as Noatak began accelerating away from the derelict ship.

"Captain?" Mek called from behind a stack of containers.

At that same moment, Noatak's voice crackled through the bay's comm. "Confirmed Syndicorp ship closing in fast. We need to burn, ASAP."

"We need five minutes," Qaiyaan said, assessing the remaining cargo.

"Captain!" Mekoryuk called again. "We have a problem."

"What?" Qaiyaan leaned around the corner. Tovik and the medic stood over a cargo box, staring down at a portal in its surface. Blinking red light bounced off both their faces.

Tovik rubbed his hand vigorously across the small window. "Is that a girl?"

"You've got to be fucking kidding me." Qaiyaan slapped a mag clamp against the container he was securing and stood. "A cryo-pod? Who the hell picked that up?"

"You said grab everything," Tovik said. He looked up to meet Qaiyaan's gaze. "Can we keep her?"

Noatak came over the com again. "Captain, they're hailing us."

Qaiyaan scowled and thrust a finger at the cryo-pod. "She's not a *netorpuk* puppy, Tovik. Just secure the damn thing so we can burn. We'll figure out what to do with it later."

"That's the problem," Mek said. "The cryo's failing. She won't survive a burn in this state."

"Fuuuck." Qaiyaan stomped over to the pod. He should have known things were going too easy. Looking at the face through the glass, his mouth grew suddenly dry. A young woman with long charcoal hair lay inside, a crescent of dark lashes against her high cheekbones. The blinking red light near her head illuminated her perfectly sculpted features as if coating them with blood.

"Just vent it," Noatak spoke over the line. "Let Syndicorp pick it up."

Tovik grabbed the end as if claiming the pod as his own. "You can't do that. What if they miss her?"

Noatak answered, "Not our problem."

"You should see what she looks like…" Tovik continued.

Now wasn't the time to argue over crew shares of the spoils, but Qaiyaan felt a sudden desire to wrestle the pod away from his engineer and claim the contents for himself. He tamped down the feeling. If they didn't get moving immediately, Syndicorp troopers would shoot first and ask questions later.

Noatak's voice boomed over his thoughts. "*Anaq*! They just obliterated the human ship!"

Syndicorp is out for blood today. Clenching his jaw, Qaiyaan shoved Tovik aside and began pushing the box toward the airlock, averting his gaze from the breathtaking face inside. "If we vent her, they'll have to stop and pick her up, which'll give us more time to get away."

"But, Captain—" Tovik started.

"We're not murderers!" Mek shouted, moving to intercept the box.

The comm filled the bay again. "Captain, you're not going to like this." Noatak's voice had gone from excited panic to deadly quiet. Qaiyaan ceased pushing, turning to face the speaker as if he could read his first mate's face from here. Noatak only used that voice when something deadly was going on. "They took out the passenger ship, too. There's nothing left of either vessel but a haze of space dust."

The breath left Qaiyaan's body. Syndicorp'd destroyed their own ship? Why would they do that?

Mek moved close to the captain, his voice low. "Venting her is a death sentence."

Qaiyaan squeezed his eyes shut. Why could nothing ever be easy? This woman was probably some scrawny human female on an exorbitant corporate cryo-vacation or some such nonsense. But he couldn't just leave her, not to the mercy of space, and definitely not to a ship that was blowing up everything in its path. "How long do you need to wake her?"

"The waking cycle takes twenty minutes."

He leveled a glare at the medic. "I didn't ask how long it takes. I asked how long you need."

Mek shook his head. "I can pull her out now, but she'll take days to recuperate. And she'll still be too weak to strap in for burn."

"Days to recuperate is better than minutes to end up as space dust. Pull her. We can link our ionic shells to protect her during burn."

Mek's right eye twitched. "We're exhausted from scavenging in zero atmo. I'm not sure we can withstand the strain."

"Do you have a better suggestion? If you do, make it now, because we're out of time."

"They'll be in range in thirty seconds, Captain," Noatak clipped out, his voice still deadly steady.

Mek's jaw bulged, but he nodded. "Fine. I think I've got enough stims to keep us up and running afterward. But let's not make a habit of it."

Popping the pod's seals, Qaiyaan knelt to lift the frigid human from the padded interior. She was naked, her nipples peaked from the cold. His hand slid beneath her nicely rounded bottom, every ionic sensor in his skin aware of the contact. He tried to remain focused on her face instead of the silky smooth curve of her hip cradled against his chest. Her eyes fluttered but didn't open.

Laying her on the deck, he stretched out beside her, grounding himself to the metal decking. Enveloping her in his power. Locking his body against hers.

Tovik sat cross-legged at her head, his bare feet tucked beneath him, and placed both his hands on her shoulders. But his gaze was on her upright nipples. Come to think of it, Qaiyaan's were, too, so he couldn't blame the young engineer. Mek spread out along her other side. An unfamiliar twinge made Qaiyaan want to shove them both away.

Hoping he hadn't just given all four of them a death sentence, Qaiyaan called out, "Engage full burn."

CHAPTER TWO

Lisa's entire body ached as if she'd been thrown down the stairs. Her muscles whimpered in pain, and she realized she was trembling. More than trembling. Freezing. *Frozen.*

Memories came back in a rush. *Hell, yeah, I survived!* Her gritty eyes flew open and her lungs sucked in an agonizing breath. Her brother, Doug had reassured her Syndicorp wouldn't hurt her as long as they needed him. And he had a way of ensuring people needed him. Still, the corp' could con even the most skilled grifter, as she well knew. If it hadn't been for Doug, she never would've agreed to be put into such a helpless situation. Stepping into that cryo-pod had been the largest act of faith in her twenty-six years of life.

Her frigid fingers tingled with renewing circulation and her eyelids fluttered as she tried to focus. Doug was supposed to be here to meet her. Her heart ached to see her twin again, to be sure the corp' hadn't hurt him. Her nano-bots must still be inert from the time in cryo, or she'd have felt him immediately.

Above her, ceiling panels glowed with dingy light. She rolled her blurry gaze to the right. A wall of compartments stood a few feet away, the dull metal clean, but not what she'd come to expect after a year as a Syndicorp test subject for nanite technology. These cabinets were part of a small ship's med bay; she'd seen her share of them over the years, mostly because her brother couldn't seem to keep himself out of bar fights.

So where was she, and why was she awake? Her journey was supposed to end at a new lab where Doug was undergoing super-secret test exercises. Something must've happened if she was out of stasis early. With effort, she rolled her gaze the other direction. A steel counter ran along the far wall, a small sink embedded at one end and a computer station at the other. A huge man sat there, three thick ropes of hair banded with metal hanging down his broad back.

Definitely not corporation.

"Nnnmm," she tried to catch his attention, but her tongue was as frozen as the rest of her.

The man looked over his shoulder, his concerned face reflecting the light as if he'd dusted with that fancy cosmetic powder the men on Enayshu Five always wore. He lacked Enayshuan eye-ridges, but he was definitely alien. "You're awake. Excellent."

Spinning his chair to face her, he thrust one bronze-sheened hand toward her throat. This close, she was struck by how huge he was. She flinched, but he merely pressed his fingertips to her pulse. Manually checking her vitals? Shit, she *was* on a low-end ship. She felt like she was back in the underbelly of Whylon Station.

"What happened?" She couldn't wrap her tongue around the gravelly words, but the man seemed to understand her anyway.

"We're not entirely sure. We pulled you off a derelict ship."

"Derelict? I don't understand. Who are you?" Her voice sounded better but still slurred.

"My name's Mekoryuk, but you can call me Mek. The captain wants to talk to you. I'll let him know you're awake."

She struggled to sit up, but her body only twitched like a dying fish. "I need to call my brother."

"You can barely form words. Stop trying to move." He pressed a solid hand against her collarbone, pinning her to the mattress. "I don't want you exerting yourself until your metabolism stabilizes."

"But I—"

Mek's hand pressed harder. "I'm going to get the captain now. If you fall out of bed it's your own *usviiq* fault."

Lisa lay still, focusing on her breathing. The pressure of his hand eased, but he kept his gaze on her, as if reassuring himself she would do as instructed. When she didn't protest, he turned and left the small bay.

For a few minutes, she simply rested, listening to the beeping of monitors and the slight hum of the ship's engine. If there was one thing Syndicorp was good at, it was keeping hold of its property. Yet here she was on a strange, very non-corporate ship. Something had gone very wrong. She didn't care what Mek said about resting; she needed information.

Inside her head, her tiny robotic nanites were stirring. They swarmed and buzzed at her temple as if curious about the diode connecting her to the med-bay monitors. She was part of a test group for "cyber-sensitive" enhancements; a way to empower human brain waves to interface directly and intuitively with complex computer systems. The nanites were designed to send and receive data impulses, using the host brain's synapses. Doug could hack into a nearby computer system with a mere thought. Lisa wasn't nearly that good and needed to be physically interfaced to hack into a system. Lucky for her, the diode provided just the corridor she needed. Hopefully, the medical computers were tied into the mainframe, and she could encode a call to Syndicorp. She squeezed her eyes closed, instructing the microscopic machines to investigate.

A voice interrupted her concentration. "How are you feeling?"

Her lids flew open to meet an electric-blue gaze. She'd thought Mek was handsome, broad-shouldered and roguish with his long, banded hair and clean-shaven face. This new fellow pushed the boundaries of rogue and headed straight to rugged, copper-skinned barbarian. His long hair flowed loosely around his shoulders, dark and wavy, offset by strands of silver that might be a metallic weave, or might be his own hair, she couldn't quite tell. Mostly because his eyes were so damned brilliant and captivating. Above those eyes, a silver loop pierced one dark brow.

Holy hell, were all the crewmen on this ship hot like this? The man's sensuous lips curved slightly upward, as if he was very used to smiling, although he wasn't at the moment. A well-trimmed mustache and beard tapered to two, tidy braids under his chin. He'd just asked her a question, but her tongue felt too thick in her throat to respond.

Mek moved around from behind the barbarian at her bedside. "She may take a while to fully recover."

The second man raked her body with a gaze that left her tingling for his physical touch. She shuddered right down to her core, confused about this unusual reaction to a man—an alien. She'd been with plenty of guys—okay, a few guys—and not a single one had ever made her feel like this, in bed or out. She was supposed to be resting, but perspiration prickled her skin as if she'd just climbed through the space station's high-grav service tunnels.

"I'm Captain Qaiyaan. Can you tell me your name?" The deep timbre of his voice sent thrilling little rockets along her skin.

"L-lisa. Lisa Moss." *Way to sound like an idiot.* She licked her lips, hoping her next words didn't come out like mud.

Qaiyaan's gaze followed the move, then flicked toward Mek, who began tapping at a polycom, probably doing a search for her profile. *Good luck with that.* Her lips twisted into a smile. Syndicorp had made sure she and her brother disappeared when they'd joined the test group, wiping their slates clean of a handful of crimes and hiding the siblings from the black market cartel that was seeking their heads.

"Lisa, we're trying to piece together what's going on. Why were you in a cryo-pod?"

Her smile dissolved. One wrong word and both she and her brother would lose everything, including the amnesty that kept them out of the Syndicorp prison mines and the cartel's hands. She blurted out the first thing that came into her head. "Interstellar Myasthenic Carcinoma."

Shit. She must still be slow from her time in cryo. No one actually came down with IMC anymore. The cancer, caused by unshielded travel through dark nebula, was a barely more than a horror story told by station rats consoling themselves for being stuck station-side.

Qaiyaan's eyes rounded a fraction and he shot a glance to his medic, lips forming a thin line. Mek straightened to meet his gaze, his face equally stricken. "I didn't detect anything during my scans. Let me check again."

She scrambled to keep him from digging further and discovering the truth. She could do this. Had pulled cons a hundred times with her brother before the Syndicorp police had reeled them in, giving them a choice between the mines and the test program. Smiling weakly, she played her pity card. "That's okay, really. I'm on my way to a hospital for treatment."

Mek started pushing buttons on her monitors. "What stage are you at?"

A thread of panic threatened her composure. She had little experience with advanced medical treatments, nanites notwithstanding. Thinking of the microscopic robots roaming her body, she sent them to interfere with the doctor's sensor. Doug probably could've faked a reading for IMC, but she wasn't that skilled. Leaving her nanites to run amok, she focused her attention on the blue-eyed man standing next to her bed. "I—I need to let my brother know I'm okay."

Qaiyaan shook his head, avoiding her eyes. "I'm sorry. Our comm isn't set up for long-range boost. You'll have to wait until we get to a transfer station."

"How long will that be?" She fluttered her fingers, trying her damnedest to regain enough coordination to touch him. To her delight, he pulled a seat over and took her hand. His skin was warm and slightly rough as his thumb grazed the back of her fingers. She shivered right down to her nanites, a million little tingling sensors responding to his touch.

His thumb stilled, as if he sensed something, too, and he stared intensely into her eyes.

Barely infringing on her awareness, Mek's fingers probed the diode affixed to her temple. "Hold still. I'm going to swap out the sensor."

She shook her head. Her rapid heartbeat was sure to raise some alarms if he got the diode working again. "Don't bother. Something about my chemistry makes standard technology go haywire. I can't even wear a polycom without it fritzing out."

"Just let him try, okay?" Qaiyaan squeezed her hand gently.

Heart racing, she gave him her "brave-but-scared" smile and tried to think like a cancer patient. "I need to get to the hospital on Aleigh right away."

Mek stopped muttering under his breath and both men stared at her.

"You were going to the Syndicorp hospital?" Qaiyaan's brows drew together.

Her chest was tight, and she was sure Qaiyaan must be able to feel her trembling. Answering a question with a question was the best way to carry a grift, Doug always said. "Don't they have the best medical technology?"

Mek made a grunting noise and returned to making adjustments on his screen. She boosted her nanites to be sure they kept interfering. Qaiyaan shifted his gaze to her fingers, his strangely bronze thumb tracing a thin blue vein on the back of her hand. "You're quite a ways from Syndicorp space."

Oops. Part of the reason they'd put her into cryo for shipment was to keep her from hacking any systems and discovering where they were taking her. She'd just assumed they'd still be in Syndicorp space. "How far?"

"Fifteen or twenty parsecs, I'd say. And a long, long way from Aleigh."

Calling on skills she hadn't used in a year, Lisa drew her brows into worried lines. "They told me I was going to Aleigh." She'd always excelled at drawing out a target's empathy, playing their emotions to get what she needed. Right now she needed Qaiyaan to stop asking questions and give her access to a comm. "My brother must be crazy with worry. What do you think happened?"

"You have to watch your back with Syndicorp."

"Don't I know it." She laughed, then realized she was being too honest. Her doubts about Syndicorp were something she kept deeply buried, even from her brother, who was their star subject. She was fairly certain she hadn't been sent to the mines or handed over to the Whylon Cartel only because Syndicorp needed him. Her skills with the nanites were abysmal at best.

Qaiyaan's fingers tightened against her hand, and he rose. "Mek has some experience with cancer, so just relax and let him do his thing, okay?"

Her heart sank. Of course Mek would be some sort of cancer specialist. Why hadn't she claimed to be going to a rehab colony or something? "Please don't go to any trouble. I've already paid Syndicorp for the treatment. I just need to get to Aleigh."

Qaiyaan moved to the door, but stopped and looked over his shoulder at her. His blue eyes were wild sparks beneath his deep brow line. "Syndicorp's probably not your best option at this point. Give Mek a chance. I'll check back soon."

With that, he was gone, leaving the small med bay strangely empty without his presence. All Lisa could do was boost her nanites to fend off the doctor's repeated scans.

CHAPTER THREE

Qaiyaan shook his head as he stomped back to the control room. With effort, he could've forced himself to stay away from the med bay and the alluring patient within. But a woman with IMC? Cancer had been all but obliterated except for the rare kinds that took hold without symptoms until it was too late. Like the kind that had destroyed his entire race. Lisa's arrival was like the ever-sneaky *Ellam Cua* had connived to taunt him—his entire crew—with memories. Even Mekoryuk was obviously taken by the human female. She was so exquisitely vibrant, despite the lingering effects of the cryo. Despite the disease eating her bones. The perfectly sculpted curves of her body beneath the thin sheet had been difficult to ignore. And when he'd touched her hand... The almost electric jolt at the connection had almost made him wonder if she was Denaidan, too.

But that wasn't possible.

Cancer had wiped every female from existence. *Syndicorp* had wiped them out. And now they were gunning for Lisa.

He hadn't had the willpower to ask her why they might be after her. Hell, they might not even be after Lisa. There could've been something on that ship the corp' wanted to hide. Syndicorp wasn't above ancillary damage—they'd proven that on Denaida-Daru. No need to upset her while she recovered. After he'd arranged for her medical attention, he'd explain how Syndicorp had destroyed her ship.

Sitting heavily in the captain's chair, he began scrolling through the star charts to line up the nearest non-Syndicorp hospitals. The galactic corporation had spread in influence and power since the destruction of his homeworld fifteen years ago. Few in the galaxy even remembered the name of Denaida-Daru, a backwater ag-planet with an indigenous population too empathically sensitive to join the rush-and-bustle of the galactic market. Denaidan women, in particular, were unable to withstand the proximity of other species' unfiltered emotions and desires, making it impossible to leave the planet; they were also the only females who could tame the intense sexual connection of a Denaidan male, a fact Qaiyaan was more aware of than usual with the charcoal-haired beauty lying in his med bay.

Jaw aching, Qaiyaan dismissed a nearby hospital as having close ties with Syndicorp and pulled up the board members of a second facility to review their names. So many companies these days were mere subsidiaries of the Syndicorp conglomerate. He kept a sharp eye on the movements of Syndicorp's CEOs and holding companies, exploiting whatever opportunities he could. The few Denaidan men who'd been off-planet during their world's destruction had formed a loose brotherhood of pirates, determined to make Syndicorp pay for their crime. The annihilation of his species couldn't be undone, but he'd make Syndicorp pay in whatever ways he could.

"Captain." The control room speaker popped with Tovik's voice, difficult to hear over the hum of the ship's engines in the background. "You there?"

"Go ahead." Qaiyaan continuing cross-referencing photos and names with his list of Syndicorp supporters, glad of the recovery stim Mek had provided after the grueling burn. Without it, he'd be laid out on his bunk right now.

"Have you found a buyer for these supplies yet? The climate control for the lower cargo bay is taking more power than I anticipated."

Qaiyaan looked up from the computer and scowled at the gauges on the control room wall. He'd forgotten about the salvaged supplies completely. Over half the inventory had turned out to be medicine, stored in cryogenic cases that were failing just like Lisa's. Keeping the fragile compounds viable until they secured a buyer had required some hack engineering on Tovik's part, and the fuel-cell gauges were flickering toward empty. Qaiyaan reassessed the star chart he'd been searching for hospitals. "How far can we get?"

"Three parsecs at full burn. Perhaps as far as the Bolisare system, but no more than that." Tovik didn't hedge his bets. What he said was the honest truth, no sugar-coating, no buffer for mistakes. "We've had to divert a lot of energy to the shields during the last three burns. That repairman on Finofan must've skimped on some of the hull platings."

The repairman *had* skimped, but it was all Qaiyaan had been able to afford. His crew had no idea how fragile this bucket-of-bolts really was—or at least they pretended not to know. He did a quick run-down of the hospital facilities within a three-parsec sphere.

Here at the edge of un-classed space, there wasn't much to be had. There was a garan'uk medical facility six and a half parsecs in, but even if the methane breathers offered services for humanoids, they were known Syndicorp allies, and Qaiyaan was a wanted man.

He widened the search. There was a Saluqan healing temple on Oruq Nine, four parsecs beyond Bolisare in another un-classified sector. If they stopped and unloaded on Bolisare, they could fuel up and get Lisa to Oruq Nine in a week or so. Did she have that long? Not that he had much in the way of options for her. Mek was a genius in his own right, but the *Hardship* lacked medical equipment, let alone medicine for humans.

Adjusting the ship's heading, he said, "We'll head to Bolisare. I'll work on finding a buyer."

"Aye-aye, Captain." The hum of the engine room silenced as Tovik ended communication.

The *Hardship's* last visit to Bolisare hadn't been an exemplary experience. Noatak'd relapsed on recovery stims and gotten into a brawl with a prominent cartel businessman. The crew'd been forced to break him out of prison. Luckily, Qaiyaan's contact on the planet was also on the alternate side of the local law. He wouldn't offer a high price for the salvaged medicine, but at this point, unloading it for cheap was better than having to jettison worthless cargo.

Feeling guilty about lying to Lisa about their comm system, Qaiyaan accessed the long-range channel for the planet's black market and sent an encoded message. The communication would take at least twenty hours to reach his contact and another twenty for a return message. By then they'd be almost halfway there. Setting the navigation controls to auto, he headed to the lower cargo bay where they kept the workout equipment. His nerves were jangling from the recovery stims, and he needed to focus his ionic energy if he was going to have a clear head for bargaining.

He also needed to keep himself from hovering over the luscious human in his med bay.

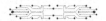

Lisa pivoted to sit on the edge of the cot and wrapped the sheet around her, her body still naked from the cryo-pod. Mek had finally left the med bay, muttering about someone named Tovik who might have a fix for his malfunctioning sensors. He was dead-set on getting a reading of her cancer, and she felt bad for putting him through so much work for nothing. But she couldn't risk exposing the Syndicorp technology. For all she knew, these men were pirates and would sell her off to the highest bidder once they found out what she carried. Her ship's demise couldn't have been a mistake. Someone was after her, and she needed to let Doug know where she was. The only way to do that was through Syndicorp.

Planting her feet on the floor, she wobbled upright. Her feet left the ground unexpectedly, and she threw out both arms to keep her balance. *Whoa.* The ship's gravity was barely enough to hold her feet to the deck. The sheet came loose and slithered down around her hips before she caught it and secured it around her breasts again. This was going to be interesting. She moved carefully toward the door. While interfering with the doctor's scans, she'd determined that the med bay computer was only attached to the internal systems, and she'd need to find one connected to the external comm to get a message out. Her head hurt from controlling her nanites to block the doctor's probes, but she'd need to use them again in short order.

Cautiously sliding the door open, she peered into the half-lit corridor. The stark wall panels were similar to a half-dozen cargo ships she'd been on. *Damn.* Some part of her'd been hoping for one of those junker ships with exposed conduit running along the walls of every corridor. Should've known better than that, based on the orderly way Mek ran his medical bay. She had to find an access panel so she could physically hack in. Or find an actual comm unit. That would be way easier. Doug could've hacked in from anywhere on the ship, the lucky bastard. He also could've accessed the ship's blueprints and known exactly where to go.

Thinking of her brother made her chest tight. If someone was after her, they could also be after Doug. He was Syndicorp's star pupil, and much more valuable than she was. She prayed he was safe and waiting for her at the corp' lab, wherever that was.

She stepped into the hall, listening for approaching crewmen. To her right, the passage ended at a closed airlock in the floor. A door across from her stood open, revealing a lavatory with a shower head in the ceiling. Left, the hallway extended maybe fifty or sixty feet toward a big bay. Closed doors to either side likely led to crew quarters. Her nanites thrummed in the soles of her feet, telling her that engineering was down the airlock to her right. At the far end of the dim hall, in the wall near the catwalk, she spotted what looked like a conduit panel. *Jackpot!*

Her bare feet slid along the metal deck, her footing unsure in the low gravity. She reached the panel and pried the metal cover loose, her fingertips stinging from the effort. Inside, cables and wires entwined each other like a nest of snakes. Tracing her fingertips along several wires, she searched for a familiar interface, skin heating and temples throbbing with effort. Damn, why did a ship need to have so many separate systems?

From behind the nearby closed door, a man's voice cut through her concentration. "She said she paid Syndicorp for medical treatment, so she has to be on the galactic net somewhere."

"Well, she isn't. Not under the name Lisa Moss, anyway."

Lisa paused her search. It hadn't occurred to her that *not* having a presence on the galactic net might be just as incriminating as her real files. Syndicorp had removed every trace of her and Doug to prevent the black market cartel on Whylon Station from tracking them down and exacting revenge. Looking back, she should've suggested arranging an "accident" to make it appear she had Doug had died rather than disappeared.

"Cryogenic containment isn't cheap," one of the voices continued. "She's got money to afford that plus what-ever she's paying Syndicorp. She probably told us a fake name to protect herself."

"Think her family will ransom her?"

"We don't know if she's Syndicorp yet. We don't target non-corp' citizens."

"I'm just saying, our hull's got to be repaired—for real this time—and this latest heist isn't enough to pay for it. Especially if the meds go sour before we get there."

Heist? Queasiness roiled at the bottom of her stomach. So these men *were* pirates. They must've attacked her ship. But if they knew about her nanites, they hadn't revealed it.

"Let me take the money to the kwirn tables and—"

"*Usviilnguq!* Last time we had to haul ass out of Bollisare so fast, I didn't get my kiss goodbye."

"The house was cheating! And your limp *ucuk* isn't my problem, Tovik."

Suddenly the door in front of her flew open, and she was looking at the broad chest of another monster of a man. Five long braids hung from his chin like tentacles, gathered at the bottom with a metal band. Her gaze followed them upward to meet a scowling bronze face.

She clutched at the sheet around her torso, stuttering out her backup excuse for wandering around. "Uh, where's the restroom?"

His gaze flicked to the open conduit panel. "Not in there."

"Sorry about that. I lost my balance and the cover fell off when I leaned against it. So clumsy." Batting her lashes, she giggled and tried to affect an innocent smile. "Don't you guys believe in gravity?"

He grasped her left biceps with a hand that felt as hard as metal. Even his knuckles gleamed like bronze ball-bearings. "I don't like eavesdroppers."

A younger man appeared in the open door, his beard a bit scruffy around the edges. "She's awake?"

"I'm not eavesdropping," she rasped out. Her racing heart was making her dizzy. "I didn't even know you were there until you opened the door."

The hand around her arm tightened. "Liar. Your pulse is going supernova."

The younger man put his hands on his hips but didn't intervene. "Take it easy, Noatak. She's our guest."

Lisa yanked her arm out of the bigger man's grip. "I want to talk to Qaiyaan."

His upper lip curled into a sneer. "Oh, you're going to talk, all right." He targeted the younger man with a glower. "Tovik, check the panel. Make sure nothing's compromised."

Once again he clasped her arm, nearly yanking her off her feet in the low gravity. He dragged her the rest of the way down the hall and onto a catwalk over a large, mostly empty cargo bay. Below, a shirtless Qaiyaan was performing a slow series of moves that looked almost like tai chi. Only his feet weren't on the floor; he stood on the wall as if gravity had lost all meaning. His gleaming copper muscles bunched and flexed in ways that made Lisa's insides quiver.

"Captain!" the man beside her shouted.

"What is it now, Noatak?" Qaiyaan jerked to a halt. He turned his head and his electric blue gaze met hers.

As if gravity had suddenly returned, he belly-flopped against the decking.

CHAPTER FOUR

Swearing loudly, Qaiyaan scrambled upright, elbows throbbing from the impact. What was the woman doing out of bed? And in his cargo bay? The thin sheet hugging her curves exposed far too much skin for a ship full of nothing but men. *And Noatak has his hands all over her.* "Dammit, Noatak, what are you doing?"

Noatak merely quirked an eyebrow. "You think I dragged her out of bed?"

"I was looking for a bathroom." Lisa struggled against Noatak's grasp.

The first mate rounded on her, and Qaiyaan was half-way to the ladder without thinking. Noatak wasn't known for keeping his temper. But the big man only spoke with deadly calm. "She had the conduit panel open. And I'm pretty sure she overheard Tovik and me talking."

Qaiyaan's primary heart sank. *Shit.* Knowing Tovik, they'd been talking about Lisa—whether ransoming her or ravaging her, neither would be good. He pulled himself onto the catwalk, his gaze hard on his first mate. "No matter what she may have overheard, she now thinks the worst of us with you dragging her through the corridors in a bed sheet. Why don't you go check our heading? I'll take her from here."

Noatak's nostrils flared, one bronze cheek twitching. "Fine," he said through gritted teeth. "Yell if you need me."

"I think I can handle a girl in a bed sheet, thank you." Qaiyaan shot Lisa a conciliatory smile. Perhaps he could play everything down. Get her back to bed...

Her face remained hard.

Qaiyaan took a deep breath and gestured down the corridor. "Why don't we see about getting you some clothing?"

Gripping the sheet over the enticing swell of her breasts, she turned and shuffled ahead of him. His gaze was drawn to the two pert mounds of her ass cheeks. Damn flimsy sheet. Why was he so turned on by her? He'd had female passengers on board before and never felt a twinge of temptation. Denaida men could never consummate with non-Denaida. The prostitutes he and his men engaged were nothing more than accouterments to masturbation; three-dimensional pornography to be viewed, smelled, perhaps lightly touched or kissed, but never used for climax. The very act would put a non-Denaidan into a coma.

Perhaps it'd been too long since he'd indulged in a release. Might she be willing to assist? His mouth nearly watered as he watched her move, imagining that sheet sliding from her curves in a sensual slither, his hands molding against the indentation of her waist. Those bare feet wrapped around his backside as he drove himself into her...

Shaking his head, he attempted to banish his rather obvious arousal. She'd suffered enough already under Noatak's brutish accusations. Not to mention she was terminally ill. How could he be so damned insensitive? He needed to keep his nether regions tamed. He walked slowly behind her, breathing deeply to re-center his thoughts. She trailed the lingering chemical scent of the cryo-pod, but underneath it, he detected a faint floral aroma that reminded him of Denaidan lilacs. *Anaq. I definitely need some shore leave.*

At the end of the hall, Mekoryuk came bursting out of the med bay, his face dark with worry. He spotted them, and his shoulders relaxed. "Oh, thank *Ellam Cua* she's all right. She shouldn't be out of bed!"

Qaiyaan shook his head at the medic and nudged Lisa toward his cabin. His palm itched against her bare skin. "She's fine. I'll have her back to you in a little bit." He guided her into his quarters, suddenly wondering at the wisdom of being alone with her in his bedroom.

Lisa entered the small space and moved immediately to the far end of the room, turning to glare at him with her arms crossed and her chin down. "You're a pirate."

The accusation pierced him, though he wasn't sure why. All he'd wanted to do was drop her at the Saluqan facility with her none the wiser about her rescuers. Be a knight in shining armor. Save a woman from her insidious disease as he'd been helpless to do with his own people. Maybe it wasn't too late. He had no idea what she actually knew versus what she merely suspected. Moving to his closet, he rifled through his few items of spare clothing. "How'd you come to a conclusion like that?"

"Don't bullshit me," she said. "You didn't just happen upon my ship floating derelict in space."

He chose his softest black tunic and a belt. His trousers would be far too long in the legs, but perhaps the shirt could serve as a dress. Turning, he held the pirelux silk up by both shoulders, assessing the length. "You're right. We intercepted a distress call."

Her full lips pursed in a scowl. "Right after you disabled my ship. Stop trying to double talk me. I've dealt with your kind before. I'll tell you right now, there's no one to pay a ransom for me, so you may as well drop me at the next space station."

There was a hardness lying just beneath her surface, a solidness he could sense in the beating of her heart, and he knew he was talking to a woman who'd been through some *anaq*. Something deeper was at stake here, something she wasn't telling him. Taking two steps forward, he offered her the shirt. "Wouldn't a pirate have jettisoned your cryo-pod the moment the Syndicorp trooper ship appeared, hoping they'd stop the chase to pick you up?"

A black scowl settled over her features, and she snatched the shirt from his hands. "Why didn't you?"

"They'd just blown your passenger ship to smithereens." He quirked an eyebrow at her and laid the belt on the desktop nearby. "I had a feeling they might do the same to you."

Her shiny dark hair had just poked through the neckline of the shirt. The scowl on her face slackened, and her creamy skin blanched bone-white. "Why would they do that?"

"That's what I was hoping you could tell me. Any reason Syndicorp might want you dead?" He sat on the edge of his bunk. While his eyes watched her body language, his ionic sense reached out to feel the nuances of her heartbeat, breathing, and skin temperature. He had nothing close to the empathic power of a female of his species, but he could still sense physical changes that might give a clue about another's hidden thoughts.

Lisa turned away from him, shoving her hands into the shirtsleeves. Her body was trembling, but her voice remained strong. "You're lying. "

"Why would I lie about that?"

"To get me to talk. To tell you my secrets, if I had any secrets." Her heartbeat spiked, telling him she likely did have secrets. The shirt hem fell almost to her knees over the top of the wrapped sheet. Still facing away from him, she picked up the belt he'd laid on the desk next to her and allowed the sheet to fall in a puddle around her ankles while she cinched her waist. Those long, sculpted legs poking from beneath the shirt's hem made him harden again.

He leaned forward with his elbows on his knees to hide his bulging crotch. "So Syndicorp *is* after you."

"I never said that. You attacked my ship and took me captive. But I'm telling you, no one will claim me." She began to roll up the too-long shirt sleeves as if she wore a man's clothing all the time.

Jealousy created a silent growl in the back of his throat as he thought of situations where she might wear another man's shirt. He took a deep breath to shove the feeling down. "And I'm telling you, we didn't attack your ship. We answered a distress call from the pirate who did. Then the Syndicorp troopers showed up and forced us to run. They destroyed everything we left behind."

Turning to him, she narrowed her eyes. "If you're not pirates, and you merely stopped to aid a ship in distress, how did my cryo-pod end up on your ship?"

"I never actually said we weren't pirates," he growled, tired of word games. He just wanted the truth out of her. He wanted her to understand that if Syndicorp was after her, he was on her side. Something she'd said in the med bay came back to him. "Why did you trust yourself to cryo if your chemistry interferes with electronics?"

A flush rose to her cheeks. "It... I'm... that's probably why it failed."

He rose and paced forward to stand over her. Even without his ionic sense, he knew she was lying. "What kind of cancer did you say you had?"

She licked her lips, her gaze sliding away, body breaking into a sweat.

"You don't have cancer." He didn't need her to corroborate his words. Beneath his palms, he felt the adrenaline flooding her system—the trembling muscles, the elevated heart rate, the shallow breathing. Even her nerve endings seemed to rise to the surface, to reach for him, telling him she was as aware of the closeness of their bodies as he was. Or perhaps that was just wishful thinking. He'd allowed himself to be manipulated by this woman. He'd made choices that endangered his ship and his crew because of her. Well, not anymore.

He clasped her shoulders and turned her to face him, her slate gray eyes wide and fearful. Good. Let her fear him. Whatever it took to get the truth out of her. "That passenger ship you were on had been gutted and filled with cargo. Even the med bay's equipment was removed. Seems to me whoever put you on board didn't care if you lived or died. Considering Syndicorp destroyed its own ship, I'm thinking they may have even *wanted* you dead. If you want my help, it's time to tell me the truth."

CHAPTER FIVE

L isa's heart threatened to beat its way out of her chest. Her secret was out. But with what Qaiyaan'd just revealed, she wasn't sure it mattered anymore. "S-Syndicorp did what?"

"They destroyed the pirate ship that attacked you. Then they moved to your ship, firing more than once. There's nothing left but space dust." His blue eyes looked into hers with an intense protectiveness she'd only ever felt from her brother. She was reminded of the time she was fourteen and had tried to con a drunken thug in a Whylon back-alley. Only it turned out he wasn't so drunk after all, and she'd found herself cornered and beaten until Doug arrived to chase the guy off. Her brother'd given her the same "what the hell did you think you were doing" look Qaiyaan was giving her now.

Still, she didn't want to believe Syndicorp might actually try to kill her. Her brother had promised she was safe as long as he was alive. "Maybe they hit my ship on accident while they were shooting at the pirate."

Qaiyaan shook his head.

She knew he wasn't lying; her nanites were reading him like lines of code. Her skin tightened into goosebumps. There was something very wrong with this story. And yet familiar. Cyber-sensitive participants who failed the program had their nanites neutralized, received a severance package, and were released. Yet they were mysteriously never heard from again. There'd been rumors the corp' was neutralizing more than simply the nanites; they were eradicating any possible leaks in the program. Although Lisa seemed to fail more exercises than she passed, Doug insisted Syndicorp would never eject her from the program. They needed her as a bargaining chip for his participation.

But what if something happened to him? If the new tests they were giving him turned out to be fatal...

She grew light-headed, stumbling toward the bed before she collapsed. *No.* They were twins. She'd know if he died, she was sure of it. She couldn't imagine life without her brother at her side. But if Doug was dead,

Syndicorp would see her as a liability. They'd ensure she was disintegrated to keep her nanites from falling into a competitor's hands. *He can't be dead!* She refused to believe such a thing.

Qaiyaan thrust out an arm to support her, lowering her to sit beside him. She gratefully leaned into his strong support, her nanites buzzing. "I need to find my brother."

"What does your brother have to do with any of this?"

She chewed her lip, contemplating how much to say. Qaiyaan was an admitted pirate, and if he knew about her nanites, what was to keep him from selling her out to the highest bidder? But she had to tell him something if she wanted his help, and the best grift was one with a whiff of truth. *Tell him about Doug's involvement. That should be enough.* Aware of his amber-and-cedar scent filling her senses, she began. "He's being held by Syndicorp as a test subject. It's top secret. *He's* top secret."

The arm behind her stiffened. "Test subject for what?"

Play the scared maiden. Swallowing, she twisted to look him fully in the eyes and let her voice tremble. "I'm not supposed to tell anyone."

"I'm no friend to Syndicorp." The menace in his voice would have been frightening if he'd directed it at her. "You have to offer me more if you want my help."

She took a deep breath. The idea of this burly copper alien acting as her protector was rather comforting. And if Doug was in trouble, she didn't have time to draw out the game. This close, she again noticed the satiny, burnished copper sheen of Qaiyaan's skin. He looked somewhat like one of the high-end cyborgs corporate bigwigs used as bodyguards. But his skin felt all-too alive where it touched hers, both a distraction and a draw. *Just offer another bite of truth, not the whole thing.* "Cyber-sensitivity. It's kind of like a psychic ability to hack into computers."

Qaiyaan made a surprised sound. "Psychic computer hacking. Interesting. How did he end up a test subject?"

"Doug was a hacker for the cartel and knew a lot of backdoors." She didn't want to go into the whole back-story of how she'd fallen hard for a cartel smuggler named Seloh, how he botched a job then tried to run. The cell leader made an example of him by torturing him to death, and she'd been unable to help. From that point on, she'd begged Doug to look for a way out. "Syndicorp offered us a deal."

"You turned on the Whylon Cartel? That's a good way to end up dead."

"I know. But it was that or the prison mines on Nunam-qa. The cyber-sensitivity testing was a sort of witness protection program."

A growl of disgust came from Qaiyaan's throat. "Slaves for the corp' or dog meat for the cartel. Either way you lose."

She shivered, thinking of what awaited her at the hands of the cartel's enforcers. Unlike Syndicorp, the cartel wouldn't send assassins—they'd send torturers. "When the doctors wanted to move him to a new secret test facility, he refused to leave without me." She sucked in a shuddering breath, realizing how much she missed him. "He and I are twins. We've been through a lot together."

Qaiyaan still had his arm around her and gave her a gentle squeeze that made her eyes prick with tears. The deeply masculine strength of him was more comfort than she'd felt in a long time. Telling the truth to this man came far too easy. *Don't fall into trusting him just because he's gorgeous*, she reminded herself. *Seloh was gorgeous, too, and look where that got him.* Keeping men at a distance kept her heart safe. Her brother was the only man who could ever know the real her.

But she didn't see much harm in what she'd revealed to Qaiyaan so far. She continued, "The doctors at the facility did everything they could to get Doug to cooperate. Then I woke up one morning, and he was gone. The doctors told me he'd changed his mind." Her heart was pounding double time as she remembered those last few days without him. "He'd never leave without telling me. Never."

"You think they kidnapped him?"

"I *knew* they had. I tried to hack into the Syndicorp systems to find out where he'd gone—where they'd taken him—but they had firewalls within firewalls, most leading to dead ends." She half-laughed. "If the situation'd been reversed, Doug could've found a way of using his cyber-sensitivity."

"That still doesn't tell me how you ended up in a cryopod on a gutted passenger ship in the middle of unclassified space."

She licked her lips, remembering that awful moment when she'd been offered a chance to join her brother. "A corp' rep called me and told me Doug was refusing to do any of the tests at the new facility until I joined him. I insisted on speaking to him, and they let me, but he couldn't say much. But he did say they would transport me if I agreed to travel in cryo."

"Why in cryo?"

Her throat and chest felt tight as if experiencing the helplessness of the freeze-chamber all over again. "If I was frozen, I couldn't access any travel logs or destinations. They want to keep the lab's location secret." In addition, the cryo had been to stabilize her nanites for space travel; not only did she suck at hacking, her nanites were what the doctors called "high strung" and didn't respond well to external stimulation, such as burn drives. But she couldn't tell Qaiyaan about her nanites. "Now I wonder if they ever meant for me to reach the lab at all. I'm worried about Doug, and I don't know how to find him."

Qaiyaan's handsome face twitched with disgust. "You can't trust Syndicorp."

"That's what I told Doug when we first joined the test program, but he said he'd do whatever it took to keep me safe." She shook her head. "He's always been overprotective."

"I would be, too." His voice was low and seductive. Attentive in a way that surprised her.

She was pouring her heart out to this man, this stranger she knew absolutely nothing about. Her gut instinct was screaming at her to confide in him—an unfamiliar sensation for a grifter who grew up on Whylon. She needed to deflect the conversation long enough to regain her balance, then she'd decide how much more to tell him. "Do you have any brothers or sisters?"

His eyes had been attentive and concerned until that moment. Now they turned stormy. Behind her, the muscles of his arm bulged with tension. "Not anymore."

"Oh." For some reason, she hadn't expected that answer. The same instinct that told her to trust him now urged her to comfort him, and she wasn't exactly the nurturing type. She placed a hand on his knee. "I'm so sorry. What happened?"

He shook his head, his braided beard sweeping his chest. "Syndicorp killed them."

Her mouth grew dry. She might have more in common with this pirate than she'd imagined. Her parents had died at a young age, leaving her with little more than vague recollections of their presence. Now she only had Doug. And if he was dead...

Before she could ask another question, Qaiyaan continued. "Syndicorp destroyed my entire race, actually."

The way he said it, so matter-of-fact, suspended her worries about Doug. "Your entire race? How?"

Qaiyaan's eyes flashed like solar flares. "A genetically modified virus that was supposed to be harmless. It caused a chromosomal mutation much like cancer in Deniadan females and spread like a plague across the planet. Every female died within months after Syndicorp began testing."

Lisa's stomach turned over. No wonder he'd been so intent on saving her. The illness was personal for him. She was usually immune to guilt, but right now shame was making it hard to breathe. Her lie cheapened his loss. The deep, almost primal part of her urging her to tell this man everything threatened to blast right through her cartel-hardened exterior. *Every girl needs a secret weapon*, she reminded herself, a mantra from her days in the station slums. Back then it had been a knife in her boot or a magnetically charged hairpin for picking locks. Were nanites really so much different? She shook off the guilt. *Keep him talking about himself.* "Why would Syndicorp infect your planet?"

"Field testing a viral herbicide." Qaiyaan's eyes grew hard and hopeless as he stared at the wall past her shoulder. "When it became apparent the virus had jumped species, Syndicorp sterilized the planet. Survivors and all."

If she'd thought the story was horrible before, now it was nearly unbelievable. Only planets with no sentient life were sterilized, most often prior to terraforming for colonization. "That's… inconceivable. Why wasn't it all over the news?"

Qaiyaan shrugged almost imperceptibly. "Syndicorp controls the media. They diverted attention to the civil war in the Pulati system and rerouted all the shipping lanes. That was fifteen years ago. The corp' made sure no one remembers the name of Denaida-Daru."

Lisa was struck speechless. There'd always been rumors of that sort of thing, but no one ever believed it. Such an atrocity couldn't happen without repercussions, could it? Backlash. Revenge. She looked at Qaiyaan again with new eyes. "You're a pirate because you want revenge."

He turned his attention to her, the deadness in his eyes suddenly sharper than any knife. "I'm going to help get your brother out of Syndicorp's hands."

A wash of relief flooded Lisa's body, so intense it sapped her strength. She sagged against Qaiyaan's arm and took a deep breath. "Thank you."

His hand slid up her back, beneath her hair to her nape, his palm warm on her bare skin. Her heart skipped a beat. Maybe it was the endorphins rushing through her at his promise of help, but his lips looked imminently kissable. She felt like celebrating his promise of help. He was a partner, at least temporarily, both opposed to Syndicorp and wary of the cartel, just like she was. She licked her lips, noting his gaze following the movement. *He wants you, too.*

Without thinking any further, she leaned forward for a kiss.

CHAPTER SIX

The shock of the human's lips contacting his own shorted out Qaiyaan's mind like a solar flare, sending fiery trails of lust through his veins. The hand he held behind her head, the one he'd placed there to sense her pulse for truthfulness, was instead inundated by her desire. His blood went from red-hot to molten, settling hard at his groin. His pants were immediately far too tight against his crotch, and he shifted, sending his body even closer to hers.

She wove her fingers into his hair, sending tingles along his scalp. Holy *Ellam Cua*, he hadn't believed it was possible for a non-Denaidan to elicit a response like this, even if it was merely physical. He groaned against her lips. He shouldn't do this. Needed to pull away, now. Unlike his men, he'd never been comfortable engaging in foreplay with a woman, knowing he'd need to stop before consummation. But her kiss... Her kiss fed his soul like a long drink of water after a trek over the Favianese desert.

Her mouth moved against his with soft insistence, and he claimed her kiss, making it his own. Perhaps a few moments of bliss wouldn't hurt. Wrapping his free arm around her waist, he drew her closer, relishing her soft body. Every part of her felt like it was meant to be pressed against him. She smelled of Denaidan lilacs and honey, warm and rich and completely edible.

Bending over her, he ravaged her mouth like a starving man, plunging his tongue into her to taste deeply. Before he knew it, she was lying back against his mattress, her breasts crushed against his chest, his hand knotted in her silky tresses. Every spot his skin made contact with hers tensed with desire and his erection was an agony of pleasure against her hip. How would it feel to plunge himself, long and thick, into her folds? It had been fifteen years since his few bungling sexual encounters with Denaidan women, but his body had not forgotten. His cock might not be able to experience that pleasure, but he could still touch her. Taste her. He could make her moan his name. What would she sound like when she came? A few intimate hours would serve him well in the lonely years to come.

Sliding a hand over the thin silk shirt, he cupped her breast, barely able to breathe from anticipation.

She, too, seemed as if she was starving. Her tongue matched his movements, flicking his teeth, stroking smoothly across his lips. Their shared breath settled deep into his chest, filling him with incredible warmth. His hand slid down her ribcage and molded itself to her waist, his thumb stroking her hip bone, highly conscious of her nakedness beneath the shirt's thin silk. More than he'd ever desired anything, he wanted to explore beneath the hem, discover her moist, hidden well, envelop himself within her heat.

As if in invitation, she arched, rolling her hips against him. He groaned again, knowing this fleeting indulgence was an illusion. He could never fully be with her. But the desire to grasp whatever he could before reality came crashing down overwhelmed him. He moved his hand back up to where a breast awaited him, nipple thrusting against the fabric. Cupping her soft flesh, he circled his thumb over the pebbled peak. The nipple grew even harder, and a whimper of pleasure escaped her. His cock jumped at the sound and his ionic senses reached toward her, seeking to envelop them in preparation for the most intimate act. The fuzzy sensation of her own resonance met him, spongy against his pressure. Inviting him to settle in. To find a home. That sexual resonance was a deep well only another of his people should be able to touch. Holy *Ellam Cua*, she was going to make him lose control.

Breaking the kiss, he lifted his head to look down on her. Her ivory skin was nothing like a Denaidan's lustrous copper, but it had a satin quality all its own. Her cheeks were flushed a delightful pink, the pupils of her slate gray eyes wide and dark as she gazed upward at him. Her fingertips stroked his jawline, tracing his beard with two delicate fingers to its very tip. The filaments there vibrated straight into his secondary heart. This wasn't normal. He wrapped a hand around her smaller one, stilling her caress so he could think straight. "You sure you're human?"

"Yes." Her breathy answer once again made his cock throb painfully. "What is your race called again?"

"Denaidan." He breathed deeply of her scent, wondering if the impossible lay here before him, both terrified and encouraged by what he was feeling. Could she be a mate? Testing the possibility might be deadly for her; during the moment of climax, a Denaidan male emitted an ionic frequency which nature had designed to cause a female of his species to ovulate. A successful match was binding. Permanent. Undeniable. The alignment required between mates was an almost spiritual thing, a combination of effort by both parties to create an empathic connection which could only be broken by death.

Unfortunately, the mating frequency destroyed a non-Denaidan partner's synapses.

Because of that, any Denaidan with any self respect denied himself the pleasure of women. Qaiyaan'd heard that men on other pirate crews didn't hold to such standards, but what a fellow captain allowed wasn't Qaiyaan's business. What remained of his people were no longer under any central governance, and each captain could choose to rule any way he chose. Qaiyaan's crew were honorable men, and that's all he cared about. He refused to endanger a female with his unbridled passion.

Lisa's fingers had resumed tickling his beard, and his eyes were about to roll back in his head. He couldn't. Wouldn't. Yet her sexual resonance brushed against him as surely as her breasts crushed against his chest. What if he was passing up the one non-Denaidan in the galaxy who might, miraculously, be a match for him? Her lips trailed fiery kisses along his jaw, working upward until the tip of her tongue prodded the corner of his mouth. He groaned. There had to be a way to test his hope. If nothing else a way to convince himself to stop. What if instead of physical consummation, which meant a loss of control, he only used his ionic power? He could throttle his frequency. Test her power to accept him. If she showed any stress at all, he'd pull out.

Taking a deep breath, he sent out a tentative pulse, releasing tendrils of power along the outer shell of her resonance. The kind he'd send a female to see if her vibrations might possibly match his. Lisa shuddered, her fingers clawing against his shoulders. Her hips rolled against him again, sending his cock into a spasm.

"God, that's good." She murmured against his lips.

He placed his mouth over hers, devouring her words. It *was* good. So incredibly good. Connecting his frequency with hers felt as natural as breathing again after a long stint in void without a suit. Still kissing her, he opened his eyes, drinking in the long lashes feathering her cheeks, the slight arch of her brows, the tiny pulse of her veins beneath her eyelids. She brought one of her legs up and hooked it over his hip, drawing him closer to the heat between her thighs. He ground against her, imagining himself sheathed by her slippery folds. Plunging his tongue into her, he sent another ionic pulse.

Her eyes flew open in shock. She stared at him, brows drawn into a questioning line.

Then her eyes rolled back into her head, and her entire body went stiff as a board.

Lisa cracked her eyes open, lips tingling and swollen from the hot alien's kisses, feeling cold where his body had been. *Why had he stopped?* Overhead, the lights of the med bay threatened to burn through her eyes straight into her brain. Qaiyaan appeared in her view, his shaggy head blocking the painful light. Concern tightened his features. "You all right?"

Her nanites boiled with nasty intensity and her head ached. Reaching a hand to her temple, she found Mek's diode back in place. She ripped it away, exhaling with relief as the pain reduced to a simmer. "What happened?"

Over Qaiyaan's shoulder, the young man with the scruffy beard—Tovik?—appeared, eyes bright with excitement. "She's awake?"

Qaiyaan frowned, ignoring the young man's question. The look in his eye was wary. "You had a seizure. Mek got his equipment working and was able to run some tests."

Uh oh. Her weak smile faltered. They'd discovered the nanites. She braced herself, wondering what came next. "What kind of tests?"

The copper-skinned doctor appeared next to Qaiyaan, elbowing the big captain out of the way. "Don't stress her. I'm not sure what sets the little buggers off." Mek lifted her eyelid and directed a bright light into her vision. She flinched and tried to twist away, but he pressed a cool palm to her forehead, holding her still. "Were you aware you're infected with nano-bots?"

She scrunched her face in discomfort, grateful when he released her eyelid. Keeping her eyes closed, she nodded. Never in her life had she regretted a grift as much as she did at this moment. These men weren't cartel, they weren't Syndicorp, and even though Qaiyaan was an admitted pirate, his history made him more vigilante than villain. *Best face the truth right now, come what may.* "They're part of the Syndicorp medical testing I was telling Qaiyaan about. I was in cryo to keep them stable for space travel."

Qaiyaan's voice cut through the darkness behind her closed lids. "You said your *brother* was the test subject."

She slit one eye to look at him. "I told you we both were."

Qaiyaan crossed his arms, seeming to fill the small room with his presence. His concentration on her was an almost physical thing. "You most definitely did not."

"I said we were both at the test lab," she said weakly. Qaiyaan'd agreed to help her find her brother, and she repaid him with a lie. Waves of disappointment radiated off him, clawing at her to soothe him, to reassure him. This big alien was not one to be coddled, though. This man was the epitome of masculinity. Her sensitivity to his mood had to be some sort of girly hormonal response. Some biological drive she'd never experienced before.

From somewhere near the door, a gruff voice said, "She probably works for Syndicorp."

Blue eyes flashing with cold fire, Qaiyaan asked, "Are you working for the corp'?"

Her ire rose. They may not have gotten off on the best foot, but she thought they'd had a pretty good conversation back in his room. And a good kiss. She didn't just kiss anyone like that. She clenched her fists at her sides. "You think I want these things in my head? I'm a slave to Syndicorp. You said so yourself."

"She's a spy." Noatak's shaggy head appeared over Qaiyaan's shoulder. "What'd they pay you to infiltrate our ship? 'Cause I can tell you now, it's not worth it."

"Pay me?" Her voice rose an octave. "They tried to kill me!"

Mek elbowed the men aside, pointing at the door. "Out, all of you. I said don't get her stirred up."

"Hey, what'd I do?" the younger man complained.

The gruff man continued to glare at her without moving. "We need answers. What if she infected the ship with those bots from her head?"

Qaiyaan closed his eyes, his chest rising in a large breath. He pointed to the door. "Noatak, if you're worried, go run some diagnostics." He opened his lids and stared at the younger man. "Tovik, isn't there something you ought to be tinkering with in the engine room?"

Grumbling, both men disappeared.

"You too, Captain," Mek said.

The urge to reach out and grab Qaiyaan's hand overwhelmed her. For whatever reason, she wanted to keep him near. Did Denaidans have a special power over women or something? She wished she knew more.

Relief washed over her when his hand gripped hers, and she wondered if he felt the same need to touch her. He must since he'd reached out, right?

"I'm not leaving." Qaiyaan opened his eyes to meet Lisa's gaze. "I need you to tell me everything you can about these nanites. The truth. Were you attempting to infect my ship?"

She fought to control her trembling lips. "The only reason I was trying to hack your ship was to contact my brother."

"So you *were* trying to hack it?" He seemed to grow several inches taller and drew back.

Lisa tightened her grip, refusing to let go. She yanked the towering captain toward her and sat up so she could glare at him more easily. "I'm carrying very secret, very expensive Syndicorp tech in my head, and my ship was just destroyed by pirates. Can you blame me for wanting to figure some shit out before blabbing the whole truth to you?"

Qaiyaan's lips thinned. "Your ship was destroyed by *Syndicorp*. Every second you're on board my ship puts my crew in danger. Are there any other details you might want to tell me before we have troopers breathing down our necks?"

She sank back against the pillows. "I didn't ask to be brought ab—"

Mek interrupted their battle of wills by pressing a scanner to her temple. Pain arced outward from the point of contact, sending her flopping back against the pillow. She released Qaiyaan's hand, pressing both palms against her forehead and squeezing her eyes shut.

"What did you do to her?" Qaiyaan bent so close she could feel his breath on her skin. The sensation cooled her pain.

She opened her eyes to see Mek holding up the scanner in submission. "Her nanites aren't something I can read without equipment. She's going to need to withstand a little pain until I have more information."

After a moment, Qaiyaan straightened, making room for the doctor to continue his exam.

Mek lowered the scanner and squinted at Lisa as if trying to read her mind. "What were you doing when you lost consciousness?"

"Kissing your captain," Lisa groused, glaring at Qaiyaan.

Qaiyaan's copper skin flushed an adorable blue-green. Lisa wished he'd come close and kiss her again. The big man stared into her eyes as if he was thinking exactly the same thing. She licked her lips in anticipation. All she should be thinking about was getting well and finding her brother, and the topmost thing on her mind was making out? What was wrong with her?

The doctor cleared his throat. "I see. Well." He focused his attention on his captain as if his words weren't for Lisa at all. "I feel it's my responsibility to warn you that having sexual intercourse with captain Qaiyaan—with any Denaidan—will kill you."

Qaiyaan made a choking noise. "I wouldn't! I didn't."

Kill me? Lisa frowned, examining Qaiyaan's broad shoulders and copper skin. The thrill of his massive erection prodding her hip and the pliable yet demanding way his lips had covered hers still coursed through her blood. She couldn't remember wanting a man that badly before, let alone an alien. "I don't understand."

"It has to do with ionic frequencies and brain waves. In the moment of climax, he would basically short-circuit your synapses." Mek's face was grim.

Lisa blinked, trying to understand. Sex with Qaiyaan would literally blow her mind? *Damn.* She wasn't sure if the tingling in her core was fear or curiosity. Probably both.

Mek returned to reading his scanner. "Qaiyaan, did you by chance test her resonance?"

Qaiyaan's answer was husky. "I thought I had it under control."

Mek shifted to access his computer on the nearby counter. "Lisa, you said you were in cryo to keep your nanites stable. Did any of the Syndicorp doctors happen to mention why?"

The headache his earlier scan had caused was rising again, and she could barely focus. Looking at Qaiyaan seemed to be the only thing grounding her. She wished he'd take her hand again. "Something about sensitivity to energy fluctuations during engine burn."

Mek twisted to look pointedly at his captain. "She's sensitive to ionic pulses."

"I get that. Believe me." Qaiyaan's brows were knit, but she no longer thought it was due to anger. He seemed… concerned? And he was fighting the urge to touch her again, she knew it. He pressed his palms against his rock-hard abs.

"But she survived." Mek raised his brows as if there was far more to his words than he was saying.

Qaiyaan's eyes widened. He looked at Lisa again as if seeing her for the first time. "How?"

"I need to do more tests."

"Wait a second," Lisa raised a hand, not sure her throbbing head was letting her follow this conversation. "Survived what? We didn't have sex."

Qaiyaan wedged his body between her and the doctor. "I won't touch her again. Just keep that scanner away from her. It obviously hurts her."

"I need more data if I'm going to keep this from happening again. Her nanites are extremely unstable right now, but I don't believe they're the problem. I have a hunch it's something deeper, perhaps like an empathic migraine." Mek shifted to one side so he could see her around his captain's body. "Lisa, I believe I may be able to regulate your synapses. Do I have your permission to try?"

Syndicorp had said her nanites weren't stable, but even they hadn't known just how unbalanced she was; Doug had secretly reprogramed them a couple of times to get things under control. Even his expert hacking could only go so far. Her mind just didn't play well with the Syndicorp technology. The thought of Mek's scanner touching her again made her want to cry. But the doctor spoke with such confidence, she wanted to believe him. Wanted to trust him. What if the problem wasn't with her nanites, but with her mind? Could Syndicorp have missed that possibility? She stretched and put a hand on Qaiyaan's hip, finding solace in the contact. "I want to try."

He turned back to look at her. "Are you sure?"

Biting her bottom lip, she nodded. She wasn't sure of anything, especially this strange connection to an alien captain. Needing Doug was awful enough. Attaching herself to Qaiyaan wasn't an option. Yet she required his help to find her brother. Whether Mek's tests fixed her or not, she needed time to think. "You should go."

Qaiyaan frowned and backed away. A moment later, he pivoted and left the room. Lisa took a deep breath and made a point of focusing on the doctor.

Mek watched him go, then lifted the diode from where she'd flung it aside and showed it to her. "I'm going to reattach this. Try to endure it as long as you can."

Lisa braced herself, just like she had during countless tests in the Syndicorp lab. "All right."

As the electric pain dug into her temple, she stared at the open doorway. She wasn't the kind of woman who needed a man in her life.

Chapter Seven

Qaiyaan paced the galley, eight steps one way, turn, eight steps back. Tovik perched on the edge of the counter watching him. Noatak sat at the table, arms crossed. His scowl had become a permanent fixture. "Are you sure it's the bond you're feeling?"

"I'm not sure of anything," Qaiyaan said. "All I know is something happened when I tested her resonance and now I can't seem to get her out of my head." The desire to be near Lisa, touch her even, threatened to block out all rational thinking. Even with her only down the hall in the med bay, he felt too far away. The disconcerting feeling inside him made him jittery, almost ill. He felt as if he'd been thrown into zero-G without his ionic shell. If this was the mate bond, he wasn't sure he wanted anything to do with it.

"But you didn't have sex with her?" Tovik asked bluntly. "Maybe you came a little bit in your pants."

Leveling a gaze at his young engineer, Qaiyaan ground out. "I think I'd remember if I had."

Noatak chuckled, rocking his chair onto its back legs.

Tovik flushed, looking at his knees while he drummed his fingertips on the counter either side of where he sat. "Okay. Have you tried to communicate through the bond?"

Qaiyaan shook his head. Some Denaidan couples were so well matched in frequency, they could speak to each other over long distances without the aid of a comm system. But he hadn't even thought of attempting to communicate. Testing Lisa's resonance instead of fucking her silly had been the most rational thing he'd been capable of.

Noatak let his chair legs thump back to the floor. "Initiating an empathic connection is the highest level of bonding, Tovik. Even most Denaidan couples could never achieve that."

"But she survived his ionic test." Tovik frowned. "I bet it's her nanites."

Noatak placed his palms flat on the table and leaned forward. "Are you saying she might be hacking into his brain?"

Qaiyaan stopped pacing.

The young man swung his gaze from the ceiling to Qaiyaan's face. "Not hacking. But the nanites could be acting as an interface for your ionic resonance. Remember when we passed too close to that dark nebula, and I had to adjust the burn frequency on the engines because it was creating a sine wave that caused headaches? Her nanites are sensitive the same way. Sensitive to *us*."

"You mean sensitive to *Qaiyaan*," Noatak added. "I don't feel anything from her except trouble."

Tovik waggled his fingers like he did when he came up with an idea about upgrading the engine. "You know what this might mean? We might be able to create mates!"

Qaiyaan rolled his eyes. Surely such a thing wasn't possible? It sure as hell didn't sound ethical. "Spoken like a true engineer, Tovik."

Noatak remained rigid, his nostrils flared. "I don't like it. A bunch of micro machines in someone's head? It's unnatural."

Tovik scowled at Noatak. "At least you guys were old enough to experience a woman before the Termination. I'm going to be a virgin my whole life. Can we at least consider the idea?"

Qaiyaan balled his fists, every muscle in his body stiff. Considering the idea meant feeling hope, and that wasn't something he was comfortable with. All hope had been crushed with the destruction of his planet. Crushed by Syndicorp. "Even if she's capable of completing a mating, we can't trust her nanites. They're Syndicorp tech."

Noatak added, "She's probably a spy. Plus she's wanted by the Whylon cartel. Let's drop her on Bolisare, trade in these supplies, and burn out of there as fast as we can."

"If she bonds with Qaiyaan, we can trust her. *Ellam Cua* created the bond so we could always be sure of our mate's integrity." Tovik nodded sagely. At twenty-two, he was the youngest of the Denaidan survivors, both on the *Hardship* and within the entire pirate fleet. The poor young man had almost no memories of his ancestral home, and only called upon their god when it suited him to do so.

"*Ellam Cua* isn't her god," Noatak inserted. "Let it go."

"But the captain said that's what this feels like."

"I have no idea what I'm feeling." Qaiyaan nearly growled in frustration. He glared at the door, imagining Mek alone with her in the med bay. Testing her. Touching her. Jealousy made his blood boil. Yet uncertainty turned him cold.

"She's not Denaidan." Noatak slapped his hand on the table with a bang. "We have no idea what might happen if he tries. What if the bond only works one way? What if Qaiyaan becomes her slave?"

If the room had been tense before, the air fairly crackled now. Qaiyaan thought back to that derelict ship. He'd originally thought it could be a trap. What if Lisa was a spy of sorts? Poisonous bait, offering the one bit of hope the Denaidan pirates couldn't refuse? She didn't even have to know about it. Probably didn't. It would be just like Syndicorp to come up with that kind of plan. And they were reportedly growing weary of Denaidan pirates nibbling at the edges of their galaxy.

Tovik's excited energy had settled, and his hands lay limp against his thighs. "I hadn't thought of that."

"Of course you hadn't," Noatak said. "Listen. I'm all for finding mates and whatever, but this girl came out of nowhere. We can't trust her or her Syndicorp nanites. We need to get rid of her ASAP."

Qaiyaan stared at the table's scarred surface. Noatak made sense. Sending Lisa on her way was probably the right thing to do. The smart thing. But the idea of parting from her caused an ache inside him. "Syndicorp blew up her ship. We should at least try to find out why."

Noatak started to argue, but Qaiyaan didn't hear him. His skin had begun to tingle and his chest burned. *She's coming.* Sure enough, Lisa's small form appeared around the door jamb. She remained frustratingly just out of range of his touch, her gray eyes slightly narrowed.

Mek appeared in the hall behind her and gestured for her to enter the room.

Still watching Qaiyaan suspiciously, she moved to the table, careful to avoid touching anyone, and sat.

Qaiyaan raised a brow at Mek in question. "What's going on?"

"I gave her some recovery stim."

"You did what?" Qaiyaan balled his fists. The stim helped a Denaidan recover more quickly after strenuous ionic exertion, but it was also highly addictive. Noatak had relapsed several times since his recovery, and Mek kept their supply under lock and key.

Lisa crossed her arms and took a shuddery breath. "I told him to."

"Why?"

Mek made some adjustments on his handheld's sensor. "I gave her the stimulant to temporarily alter her brain waves. I want to gather her responses to environmental input. Noatak, touch her hand."

Noatak did a double take and stepped back, while Qaiyaan stiffened, entire body tense with... jealousy? "Why does he need to touch her?"

"I'll touch her," Tovik held out a hand. But he kept a wary gaze on Qaiyaan.

Twisting in her chair to face him, Lisa stretched out her arm and brushed her fingertips against Tovik's. Qaiyaan's pulse thundered in his ears. He kept his focus off Lisa and instead bored his gaze into the doctor, who still looked down at his handheld.

"Huh," was all Mek said, then looked expectantly at Noatak.

Noatak crossed his arms tightly over his chest, his face hard. "For all I know, she's contagious and now you're all infected. I'm not touching her."

"If we're infected, you are too. You already touched her when we caught her in the corridor," Tovik offered helpfully.

"Fine." Noatak dropped his arms to his sides. After a brief hesitation, he stretched one index finger toward Lisa, allowing her to press her fingertip against his in a strange sort of greeting. The first mate's lip curled and he pulled his hand away. "Satisfied?"

"Why are we doing this?" Qaiyaan grumbled, hating watching his crew manhandle her.

Lisa straightened her shoulders and met his gaze with an intensity that made him wonder if she possessed ionic powers of her own. "I refuse to let these things ruin my life. If I'm going to join your crew, I need to get them under control."

Join my crew? That was the last thing Qaiyaan expected to hear. A woman on board his ship? Permanently? *Anaq*, he wasn't used to being around women, let alone one as determined as Lisa. How could he keep his urges throttled if she was parading herself in front of him every day? "I, uh..."

Noatak moved shoulder-to-shoulder with him, creating a wall. "We don't need the likes of you getting in the way of our operations. Now go back to the med bay before we throw you in the brig."

"You have a brig?" Lisa's eyes widened.

Qaiyaan glared at his first mate. "No. We don't."

Mek waved his scanner at Qaiyaan. "Your turn to touch her."

A small thrill raced up Qaiyaan's spine, and through the air, he felt Lisa's matching shiver. Were they so in tune with so little effort? He didn't know how that could be, but it was a far better sensation than the vertigo he'd been experiencing in her presence earlier. Holding out his hand palm up, he allowed her to settle her small fingers over his in the lightest of touches. The thrill coiled into a knot deep in his belly. To his delight, a flush rose into her face.

Tapping a few filters on his screen, Mek looked up, his clean-shaven face alight with discovery. "Her brain waves show a remarkable similarity to Denaidan empath response markers. If I can get my hands on some supplies on Bolisare, I believe I can stabilize her synapses."

Qaiyaan exhaled, long and slow. He'd been more worried about her than he'd admitted, even to himself. "That's great news."

"And just how are we supposed to pay for these supplies?" Noatak was glaring at Lisa. "Our payload's barely going to bring in enough to get us to the next spaceport."

Lisa cleared her throat. "Mek explained the situation, and I have a proposal. The cartel has a contact moonside who launders money, provides supplies, all that sort of stuff. He can probably even get your hull fixed. He uses codes to charge to the cartel. "

"I thought the cartel wants you dead?" Qaiyaan asked.

"They already think I am. I doubt they're actively looking."

Noatak approached the table opposite her and slowly pulled out a chair to sit, his previously aggressive aura mellowed. "I take it you know the codewords?"

Qaiyaan, too, was torn between caution and the desire to fix his ship. "More important, are you sure your code-words are still good? You've been gone awhile. What happens if you give a bad one?"

"The cartel is inherently lazy, and hardly ever changes them. No one dares misuse cartel resources for fear of retribution." Her heartbeat fluttered through Qaiyaan's link. "But I won't take any chances. Get me close enough to one of their computers, and I can check they're still valid before we use them."

"With your nanites," Qaiyaan finished.

She nodded.

Tovik hopped off his perch on the counter and pulled out the chair next to Lisa, adoration in his eyes. *Great. She was turning half his crew into lovesick puppies.* Qaiyaan gave the boy a look and Tovik moved down one seat.

Tovik put his elbows on the table and leaned in. "I say we try."

Qaiyaan took the chair at the head of the table, directly to Lisa's right, where he could pick up her subtle lilac scent. "I'm not sure I like this plan. How are we supposed to get you close to a cartel computer?"

She smiled. "It's been a while since I've worked a grift, but give me a sexy dress, and I think I can get close enough. Our contact runs the kwirn tables at the Solar Swan. I'll be just another girl looking for a man with money."

Noatak groaned and rolled his eyes. "We're not exactly welcome on that side of the planet."

Tovik snorted. "I'll say. I wonder if they still have your wanted poster posted at the spaceport?"

Glad for any diversion from thoughts of Lisa in a sexy dress, Qaiyaan let out an exasperated breath and glared at Noatak. "I knew I should've left your sorry hide to rot in that prison cell."

Lisa looked from one man to the other. "Well, I don't necessarily need any of you to go with me. Drop me off near the city and I'll check things out and report back."

A heartbeat of silence, then Noatak asked, "What's to keep you from turning us in for the bounty?"

She laughed. "I'm a wanted woman myself. How would I collect a bounty?" Taking a deep breath, she said, "But I'm not doing this out of the goodness of my heart. I need you to help me pull my brother out of Syndicorp clutches. Then we can talk about pay to join your crew. A couple of cyber-sensitives can be pretty useful in a heist."

Qaiyaan couldn't help the grin cracking his lips, and he was pleased to note the same grudging appreciation cross his first mate's face, as well. Tovik and Mek simply stared on with adoring eyes. She'd fit in well if she continued to hold her own against Noatak. Damn it all if he wasn't going to get off Bolisare with a reinforced hull, a belly full of fuel—and a woman at his side.

CHAPTER EIGHT

Beneath the pale blue light of Bolisare's second sun, Lisa lowered herself into the rickshaw, feeling Qaiyaan's hungry gaze on her exposed thigh before she drew her leg inside. To be fair, she'd let the supple fabric fall open along the side slit and perhaps allowed her leg to linger too long outside the carriage as she arranged her seating. But she liked his gaze on her. Liked the way he hovered nearby and seemed to anticipate her every need before she even realized she had the need herself. For instance; this dress. He'd somehow known her exact size and procured the lustrous gold garment while offloading the medical cargo to a buyer on one of Bolisare's moons. She pulled the sleek fabric inside the rickshaw and scooted over so he could slide in beside her.

"How'd you get hold of a dress like this so quickly?" she asked.

"I used the ship's 3-D printer." His gaze kept slipping toward her cleavage.

"You printed it?" She raised her brows. Many ships were equipped with manufacturing printers, pre-programmed with blueprints for ship parts and basic necessities. Cocktail dresses weren't usually on the list of plans, let alone garments of varying sizes. "Who designed it? It fits me perfectly."

He looked away as if just realizing he'd been staring. "A captain has to be adept at everything."

That surprised her. "A pirate with a passion for clothing design?"

His copper skin flushed blue-green.

She laughed at his discomfort. She'd grown up among the diverse cultures on Whylon station and had never found an alien attractive until now. This big copper-skinned alien delighted and confused her. He was every-thing she'd ever defined as masculine; it wasn't fair that he was off limits.

Qaiyaan draped his arm over the back of the seat to make room for his massive frame on the bench beside her. He'd dressed in a sleeveless white tunic that made his copper arms look massive. Even the slightest brush of his skin against hers sent shivers of pleasure deep into her bones. Rational or not, she wanted Qaiyaan more than she'd ever wanted any man in her entire life, including that cartel thug, Seloh. She'd survived Qaiyaan's ionic test, which according to Mek should have turned her into a vegetable. Didn't that somehow make her special? Her nanites were the source of so many problems—what if they were also the solution? If she was going to be part of his crew, she was going to have to find a way to get him out of her system.

The rickshaw bumped forward, jarring her thoughts to the here and now once again. The six-legged yanipa-nimayu driving the vehicle pumped furiously against the pedals to carry the rickshaw's weight up the hill toward the Solar Swan. The casino presided over the town in a garish display of flashing neon lights. The rickshaw bumped and chattered over the uneven road; Bolisare wasn't an official part of Syndicorp, so the planet didn't receive the extensive transportation funding of classified worlds. The port was barely maintained by a hodge-podge of shippers and traders, both legit and not. The mishmash of aliens and humans, wealth and poverty was almost as richly diverse as Whylon Station.

"So, what's this guy look like?" Qaiyaan asked as they passed a billboard that read *What happens on Bolisare, stays on Bolisare.*

"He's a posungi who goes by the name Nupnup. Supposed to hang out near the tables most of the day."

Qaiyaan made a noncommittal noise, but he pulsed with worry. "You ever talked to a posungi before?"

She knew what he was really asking. Posungi were an egg-laying species, but the males were known for their appreciation of sexual interludes with warm-blooded partners. She chuckled. "Once he thinks I'm a cartel agent, he won't ask me to do anything outrageous."

The rickshaw made a sudden turn onto a side street, throwing her against Qaiyaan's ribs. He wrapped his arm around her shoulders, sending jolts of pleasure across her skin. "How are you supposed to identify yourself to him?" he asked.

"I'll ask if he knows a place to rent a cottage. He'll ask if I want blue or yellow. I'll answer turquoise, with three bedrooms and an ocean view."

Qaiyaan frowned. "That's it?"

She shrugged. "Never said it was complicated. The number of bedrooms lets him know which cartel sect to charge his services to."

Shaking his head, Qaiyaan returned to watching the crowds as the rickshaw whipped past.

They arrived at the massive front archway of the Solar Swan, a concrete structure covered with huge electronic billboards instead of windows. The arch's open doors were purely ornamental, the hinges twined with thousands of multi-colored lights.

Qaiyaan disembarked, holding out a hand to help her rise from the seat. His dark trousers molded to his chiseled thighs, rippling with every flex of muscle. The toes of his gleaming, knee-high boots were coated with a layer of dust from Bolisare's filthy streets. His clean, well-cut frame was even more appealing because of the two braids spilling from his chin and the wild mop of hair loosely bunched into thick locks about his shoulders.

She took his hand, insides quaking at his touch. Standing, the top of her head didn't even reach his shoulder.

A passing woman's manicured brows raised in appreciation. "Nice bodyguard."

Lisa grinned and looped her arm through Qaiyaan's. Together, they sauntered inside, the windowless interior lit in a raucous display of colors from the many slot machines and other low-end gambling opportunities. She looked around for the kwirn tables. She'd never been to Bolisare. Luckily, Qaiyaan seemed to know exactly where to go, urging her past the buzzing, whirring, chiming machines to a hallway on the other side of the bar. He leaned close, his voice a tickle in her ear. "See him?"

She shook her head, mouth suddenly dry as a pair of gold-scaled rakwiji stalked past her, their dorsal spikes tipped black with what she hoped wasn't blood. Rakwiji were the cartel's preferred bounty hunters, the most ruthless species in the galaxy, and always traveled in pairs. Torture was part of their mating system, the thrill of another being's pain a stimulus for the couple's sexual pleasure. Rumor had it that Seloh's death had resulted in a litter of three offspring for the cartel's Whylon Station pair. She still couldn't view the aliens with any sort of forgiveness. Suppressing a shudder, she kept walking.

The hall opened up to a room peppered with downward funnels of light illuminating regularly spaced tables. Among the games, she spotted the usual assortment of cards and dice, two attahat wheels, and finally the kwirn tables with their stacked glass betting shelves and hexagonal playing pieces. She squinted into the dim spaces between the tables, searching for the orange tentacled face of a posungi. She found her quarry bending low beneath one of the lights to swipe a three-fingered hand over the betting shelves.

Nudging Qaiyaan, she thrust her chin in the posungi's direction, then pointed toward the bar. "Why don't you go get a drink? I'll signal if I need you."

Through the elastic connection that seemed to be growing stronger between them the more time they spent together, she felt a protective wash of energy. But to his credit, he didn't argue. "Be careful."

Lisa pushed her shoulders back and sashayed through the room, stopping at an attahat table to laugh at some inane joke, then pausing long enough at a hand of black-jack to pretend to make up her mind not to play. If she made a show of heading straight to the posungi's table, he'd be on his guard. As she approached, she surveyed Nupnup's short, thick torso for indication of where he kept his polycom. Her pulse roared in her ears and her nanites were making her skin itch as she grasped at her strands of courage. She'd probably only have time for a brush of her hand to hack into his tech. One shot. And she sucked at speed-hacking.

She stopped at the opposite corner of the table and pretended to be interested in a human who was obvi-ously losing. This part she could do; the slow, lazy grift that made a man—or a posungi—think whatever she suggested had been his idea. The human grinned at her and put an arm around her waist to pull her close. "Hey, baby. You here to be my good luck charm?"

The human stank of too much Saluqan gin and his hand slid from her waist to the undercurve of her bottom too quickly. From across the crowded room, she felt Qaiyaan bristle. Damn. He wasn't helping here. Working hard to remain outwardly friendly, she leaned into the human, affecting a sultry voice. "You don't seem like the type of fellow who needs luck."

He drew himself straighter and looked around the table as if he'd just won the round. "Damn straight."

The players placed their bets, and cycled through another complicated round of moving pieces from shelf to shelf. When Nupnup swept her human's piece off its shelf, she let out a disappointed hum and pulled away in exaggerated disdain.

"Don't worry, baby." The man tried to pull her close to his side again. "I got plenty of money. Why don't you come up to my room and I'll dig into my stash?"

She raised an eyebrow and shot a glance around the table in silent, communal derision of the loser. The other players, including two men and a finofan who'd painted his ear frills a garish yellow, chuckled at the human's expense. Turning up her nose, she extricated herself from the man's grip and sidled around the table toward the posungi. "You seem to know what you're doing. Why don't you tell me which one of these lovely men is the best player?"

His second set of eyes blinked out of sequence with the others, and his lower tentacles lifted in the equivalent of a shrug. "They are all inferior to a posungi."

She smiled at him and leaned in, stroking a hand along his arm. "I love a man who's confident in his game."

He emitted a raspberry of appreciation and let all four eyes rake her body from head to toe. "I enjoy a woman who knows how to play, as well."

The double entendre wasn't lost on her, and she giggled, pressing her body to his, searching for the electric signature of a polycom. She had to hold her revulsion in check as his three-fingered hand drummed excitedly against her hip. It didn't help that she also felt Qaiyaan's low boil of rage from across the room.

She sent her nanites in search of the nearby frequency of Nupnup's polycom, but there was a lot of low-level noise from other gadgets in the room. Syndicorp had made her and Doug practice homing in on a single electronic signature too many times to count, but she'd always found ignoring the other signatures difficult.

Snuffling close to her ear, Nupnup made a joke. She laughed at it without actually hearing. *Dammit, where's his device?*

To her relief, he let her go long enough to lean over the table and set his pieces on the shelves. She concentrated harder, her nanites buzzing through her veins and making her muscles tremble. With a jolt, she located his polycom's frequency. The sudden flow of information made her legs weak, forcing her to lean heavily on the posungi. Not that he minded. His arm torqued around her, fingers digging into her ass cheek. His tentacles waggled close to her face, one making contact with her lower lip. Only years of practice at the grift kept her from shuddering in revulsion. Her nanites were collecting data as fast as they could, throwing it at her in an indecipherable wave. She needed a few moments to interpret.

Qaiyaan's resonant voice behind her made her stiffen. "There you are."

The posungi's roving fingers halted and he stared over her shoulder. "You are looking for me?"

Lisa turned, pulse thundering. The pirate captain stood facing them, his stance wide and his arms crossed over his broad chest. The waves of emotion rolling off him mingled with the data stream from Nupnup's device, further confusing her. Mentally, she begged him to back off. She wasn't ready.

"I hear you can rent me a cottage," Qaiyaan said, staring down his nose at the much shorter alien.

Nupnup belched out a breath, fluttering his chin tentacles. "You need it immediately? I'm busy at the moment."

Qaiyaan nodded curtly, his gaze flicking over Lisa as if just noticing her for the first time.

With glee, she located the file with the encrypted cartel information and fumbled with the code.

The posungi's grip on her slackened as he turned to face Qaiyaan, but didn't fully release. "You have a color preference? Blue? Red?"

Lisa's vision danced with an overlay of information, and she found the directive with the cartel codewords. They hadn't changed. Relief flooded her. Looking at Qaiyaan, she nodded imperceptibly.

His chin lifted, gaze never leaving the orange-faced posungi. "It has to be turquoise. With an ocean view and three bedrooms."

Nupnup's arm dropped from her waist. He straightened. "Three bedrooms? Are you certain?"

A flicker of indecision only she could feel tickled the air, but Qaiyaan nodded firmly. "That's my requirement."

This time, Lisa caught a strong whiff of indecision from the posungi. She stepped back, unsure what to make of that. Had the physical contact with the tentacled alien made her start to bond with him now? She shuddered in disgust. No, she was just out of practice with grifting, and Qaiyaan had an abnormally strong effect on her senses.

Nupnup's tentacles writhed. "If you are sure. Let us find a place we can discuss what you require."

Without a glance back at her, Nupnup moved off into the recesses of the Solar Swan, Qaiyaan trailing close behind. She knew better than to follow without an invitation. Besides, all this exercising of her nanites had given her an idea. She was a hacker, and weren't her nanites simply little computers themselves? Doug had reprogrammed them a few times for her when the lab tests overwhelmed her. But what if she could do it herself? She could program a few to hack into the others, and perhaps re-write their code to protect her from Qaiyaan's resonance.

Then she and pirate-captain Qaiyaan could have a little fun on Bolisare after all.

CHAPTER NINE

Qaiyaan followed the posungi to a small room behind the bar, where the orange alien sat on a high backed wing-chair that had seen better days. A small table beside him held a decanter and two glasses, but he didn't offer refreshment. A second, smaller version of his chair faced him; too small to be comfortable for Qaiyaan, so he remained standing. To the left, a large mirror dominated the wall, and when Qaiyaan sent an ionic pulse in that direction, he sensed someone watching from behind the one-way glass. He'd dealt with aliens like Nupnup before. Much of what transpired would be bluff and bravado. He'd expected no less.

Keeping his face passive, he waited as Nupnup reviewed the list Mek had put together. Finally, the tentacle-faced alien looked up. "You are requesting many specialty medical items. What do you need them for?"

"No questions asked." Qaiyaan reiterated what Lisa'd said about the contact.

Nupnup made a small, disappointed noise. "Your ship is quite antiquated and will require special considerations for repair. That may take some time."

Scowling, Qaiyaan crossed his arms and glowered down at the alien. "Are you calling my ship junk?"

Nupnup wriggled a tentacle in dismissal. "I would never call a captain's ship junk to his face."

Qaiyaan grit his teeth at the sideways insult. "How much time?"

"I can procure the medical items and send them over this afternoon. But I cannot estimate the hull repair until my man has looked at it." He ran one tentacle over his blubbery lips. "Tracking down the appropriate parts might take a solar week. Perhaps you would like to rent a room?"

Using his ionic senses, Qaiyaan assessed the alien's heartbeat, breathing, and skin temperature. He'd had limited dealings with posungi, and without a baseline, it was difficult to interpret Nupnup's integrity. He seemed calm enough. But Qaiyaan's black market dealings made him wary. *What other choice do you have?* "Just get me what I need and I'll be out of your hair, uh, tentacles."

The posungi's four eyes seemed to wink at him. "I'll send someone over to assess your ship's requirements."

"The sooner, the better." Qaiyaan spun and left the small room.

Back in the casino, he scanned the floor for Lisa. A garan'uk trundled past in its mechanized methane tank, blocking Qaiyaan's view. Dodging right, he headed toward a glint of what appeared to be gold fabric near the bar. He cleared the attahat wheel only to discover a rakwiji talking loudly to the bartender, sharp teeth reflecting the nearby neon lights. Lisa was nowhere in sight. *For Ellam Cua's sake, where'd she go?*

Earlier, as she'd moved across the room, he'd nearly busted out of his skin with jealousy, aware of every set of male eyes drawn to her swaying hips. She'd played the patrons like a pro, pausing with just enough of a smile near one table, then laughing at a stupid joke at another. Once she reached the posungi's table, he'd been relieved the ordeal was almost over. But then she'd latched onto that smarmy human for an entire round before moving to the target. By the time Nupnup had his tentacles all over her, Qaiyaan'd been at his wit's end. He knew he'd moved in too fast, but he couldn't take it anymore. He figured he could stall the guy long enough for her to get her reading, and he'd been right; she'd sent him the very clear and distinct body language to proceed.

Her cyber-sensitivity was going to make his crew a lot of money, plus, she knew the black market underground probably even better than he did. She'd be a valuable member of the crew—if he could keep himself from ripping her clothes off and finishing what she'd started back in his cabin. The hard-on he'd been fighting for the last two days had only grown more persistent with time. She had a keen wit, and a body any man would die for. Then she'd put on that dress…

You just need some time to get used to her. But he had a hard time believing anything about Lisa would ever become mundane or ignorable. While he searched the room, he tapped his cochlear implant. "Tovik, someone'll be arriving to evaluate the hull for repairs. Keep an eye on him."

"Aye-aye, Captain," The voice in his head replied. "How long you going to be?"

"Not sure. I'll let you know."

Moving down the hall toward the slot machines, his ionic senses grew desperate, yearning to call out to her. He hadn't thought to set up a rendezvous point in the event they were separated. A true mate-bond would come in very useful right now, enabling them to talk, no matter how far apart. Not that he had any hope of that, with her or with anyone.

He took a deep calming breath and kept looking. Spotting the shimmer of gold fabric near the slot machines, he discovered Lisa flirting with two young finofans. He paused, watching her throw back her head and laugh, obviously fake. But the finofans were falling over themselves to touch her, their fluorescently-painted ear fins fluttering with aroused excitement. One leaned in close to her to whisper something in her ear, and a heated surge of jealousy—a sensation he was becoming all too familiar with—flooded his limbs. Then he saw her fingertips dip into the male's pocket and extract a key. *What the hell's she doing?* The one thing he didn't need was a repeat jail-break like he'd had to do when Noatak'd fallen off the wagon with those recovery stims.

He marched over, towering above the young aliens, and glowered down at them. "This female's mine. Beat it."

The finofans cowered, ear fins flattening against their skulls, then scurried away without a sound. Lisa chuckled low in her throat. "Just in time," she said, taking his hand.

Before he could question her about the key, she was leading him to the elevator. Inside, he turned to her. "Want to tell me what you're up to?"

"Play along." Her gaze flicked to a high corner of the car and she wrapped her arms around his neck. Over her head, he spotted the camera. Who was she concerned was watching? Before he could tell her no, her mouth was on his, her tongue pressing between his lips and lighting his blood on fire. Every atom of his being surged with desire, polarizing toward her. He'd been dreaming of this since his cabin, the flavor of her filling him, floral musk and sweet feminine skin.

Her soft body molded against his hard one, and a shudder ran through her. He was sure she felt it, too, this hunger and volatile urgency. This wasn't a performance for the camera. This was real, primal. He splayed his palm against her lower back, fingertips electrified against the skin exposed by her dress's scooped back. Her hands clawed into his shoulders as if hanging on for dear life.

Taking several measured breaths even as he tangled his tongue with hers, he reined in his urge to nudge her, tamping down his ionic power and walling it up.

Instinct battered against those walls, weakening his resolve almost as quickly as he gathered it.

To his relief, the elevator chimed. Her lips swollen from the bruising kiss, she blinked glazed eyes. Her voice emerged a husky whisper. "Our floor, I think." She broke the embrace. "This way."

His skin ached in the void where her body had been, urging him to reach for her, to draw her close. He balled his hands into fists and followed her. This couldn't go any further. He knew that. But his ionic power roiled inside him like a class five hydrogen nebula.

They reached the room and the door opened in a warm rush of air, temperatures fit for finofan comfort. He breathed deeply, the change a welcome distraction. Inside, the standard decorations included two double beds and a vid-screen view of a pink sunset over deep golden mountains. She gestured him inside then secured the lock, turning to press her back against the door panel. "So? How'd it go?"

He moved to the bed and sank heavily onto the mattress. The kiss *had* been for the camera. He was relieved yet still clamoring for her touch. "I'm not sure I trust that Nupnup fellow."

"You shouldn't. He might not be cartel, but he works for them." She moved toward the replicator console on the wall. "Tula cream cocktails on ice. Two."

Qaiyaan couldn't keep his gaze from her well-rounded curves or the long swath of leg peeking from the gown's slit every time she moved. He'd done far too good a job designing that dress. That's what came of years enduring "look-don't-touch," he supposed. "He's sending the medical stuff Mek needs for you. The hull repair may take a week."

Looking over her shoulder at him, she frowned. "A week? Mek thought you needed a simple patch or something. Is the damage that bad?"

"I try not to alarm my crew. But yeah," he answered truthfully. There was no reason to keep secrets from her. "We've been about to bust a seam for a while now."

"I guess that means we have some time to kill, then. Courtesy of my finofan friends." Grinning, Lisa retrieved the drinks and offered one to him.

He gratefully sipped the icy cocktail. The smooth, buttery flavor of tula fruit and cream washed over his tongue. She sipped hers, and he watched the lines of her throat tighten while she swallowed. Damn, this woman was the most alluring thing he'd ever seen. "What if they come back?"

"Don't worry." She set her drink on the bedside table and moved to stand between his knees. "Those fellows won't find a hook-up for hours with the lines they're using."

Her musky lilac scent flooded over him and once again his cock stirred. Even if he hadn't been able to sense her matching arousal through her resonance, it was obvious in the hardened nipples outlined by the thin fabric of her gown.

She ran a fingertip down his cheek and along his bearded jaw. "I want to try something."

His heartbeats sounded like full-thrust engines roaring in his ears. "We can't. You know we can't."

She tilted her head. "We kissed in the elevator and I'm okay."

He licked his lips, remembering. "I had my guard up."

"So did I."

That made him pause. "What do you mean?"

"I've been hacking my own nanites."

He blinked, confused. "You can do that?"

"That's what I want to test." She reached down and picked up his hand, placing his palm between her breasts over her fiercely pounding heart. "If I'm going to be a member of your crew, we have to learn to be around each other."

Exactly what he'd been thinking. And if she could fix her nanites… He took a deep breath of her delicious scent. If she joined his crew, he'd eventually find himself touching her. May as well test it now instead of once they were in deep space. "It could be deadly."

Her mouth twisted into a playful smile. "It could be fun. One kiss."

He groaned and closed his eyes. He was thinking of more than a kiss. He was thinking of sheathing himself inside her, feeling the quiver of her body around him. Was she sending this emotion? It didn't matter. If she was asking, he'd give whatever she wanted. Opening his eyes he slid his palm from between her breasts to rest over her throat. Her pulse throbbed beneath his finger-tips. "One kiss."

Lisa's nanites jittered in anticipation, heightening her awareness of Qaiyaan's touch. Her *desire* for his touch.

She wanted his hands all over her body. The danger involved only heightened her arousal. *Just remember to keep tabs on those nanites.* The kiss in the elevator had proved to her that her reprogramming was working; the nanites could match Qaiyaan's dangerous frequencies.

He rose to his feet, towering over her, the heat of his muscular chest a hairsbreadth away. Her nipples hardened at his nearness. When he bent his head to capture her mouth the kiss stole her breath. Rockets of desire raced down her body and pooled between her thighs. If this was how close he could bring her to orgasm with a kiss, what would sex with him feel like?

She melted forward until her breasts made contact with his solid chest. His hand snaked around her backside to bring her toward him, his erection thick and insistent against her. The jolt to her nerves from the touch made her dizzy. *No passing out.* She bolstered her nanites, much the same way she'd done to resist the doctor's scans, and the dizziness subsided. Elation rushed through her. *You can do this.*

Raising a leg around Qaiyaan's hips, she shivered in anticipation as his cock pulsed and twitched against the thin fabric of her panties. His lips broke from hers only enough to murmur, "Okay?"

She nodded furiously and drew her other leg up, locking her ankles behind him.

He turned and dropped them both onto the bed, his weight above her a hot, pulsing mass of desire. She cupped his bearded face with both hands, her mouth as hungry as his, their tongues and lips tangling and dancing, each trying to devour the other. Her dress had been pushed almost to her waist, and his hand found her thigh, skimming up to cup her bottom. His rock-hard chest crushed against her aching breasts, and her panties were soaked where his erection pressed between her legs.

Broad palm massaging her hip, he worked his way up her side until he reached a breast. His breath caressed her cheek and throat as surely as his hand caressed the soft mound beneath her gown. Trailing kisses along her jaw, he sucked at her throat while massaging her aching breast, thumb circling her areola, teasing her into an aching peak. Then he dipped down and eased her free of the gown's low neckline, revealing her tender flesh to his tongue and the delightful tickle of his beard. She moaned, arching upward to meet him as he nipped and suckled her nipple. His other hand slipped between their bodies and cupped her sex, massaging her through her panties.

"Take them off," she begged.

He slipped his fingers beneath the fabric and stroked a finger along her slick cleft before plunging it inside. She cried out, bucking against him. He pulled out in a long, slow agony of pleasure. Raising her hips, she begged for more. Still sucking her nipple, he slammed into her again, his palm connecting with her clit. The electric jolt from the contact arced straight to her core.

Qaiyaan groaned and wriggled his thick finger deep inside her, grinding against her outer lips as she squirmed. His other hand hooked the neckline of her gown and the fragile garment parted down the front. Tongue tracing a searing path along her ribs, he lapped and sucked his way across her belly while his fingers continued a rhythm deep inside her. Then he tore her panties away and buried his face between her legs.

His mouth worked her swollen nub until hot flashes of pleasure ripped through her. His tongue, oh his tongue! Her hands wound themselves into his mass of hair as he circled her clit, his fingers plunging inside her with a friction that was rapidly bringing her to the brink of climax. She bucked and arched against him, wanting more, wanting his cock. He kept teasing the sweet spot he'd found deep inside her with his finger. The pressure built fast and hot until her entire body trembled with desire.

"Yes, Qaiyaan!" she cried, her head thrashing back and forth.

He picked up speed, adding a third finger, stretching her in an agony of pleasure. Her pulse raced so fast and hard, she thought she might actually have a heart attack and die. Pressure deep in her belly swelled, hovered. His hand that had been toying with her breast moved down to push gently on her lower abdomen, increasing the pressure of his fingers inside her.

The added sensation sent her tumbling over the edge. She screamed, her pulsing epicenter shooting mind-numbing waves of pleasure outward to her head and toes and every part in between. Never in her life had she experienced anything so intense. Her nanites were like streams of fire in her blood, lighting up every nerve ending as if the very universe couldn't contain their power.

The orgasm went on and on, longer than any woman had a right to come. The tiniest part of her realized she was in trouble a bare flicker before the world began to spin. She reached for her nanites, knowing it was too late. A program crash had begun. *Not again!*

Qaiyaan loomed over her, his copper-skinned face lined with concern. "Lisa?"

Clinging to consciousness, she blinked up at him. Put her fingertips to his cheek. Then everything faded to black.

Chapter Ten

With Lisa light as a twig in his arms, Qaiyaan shoved through the crowded casino as if the building was on fire. Local medical assistance wasn't an option—Bolisare was all but a pirate planet, and word of her nanites would expand like a supernova. He'd called Mek, who'd told him to stay put, but there wasn't a moment to spare. Qaiyaan could get Lisa to the ship faster than the doctor could gather his equipment and flag down a rickshaw. What were those bastard Syndicorp nanites doing to her right now? He felt for her pulse again, reassured by its steady beat yet terrified about what was happening to her mind.

He'd been so proud of himself back in the room, remaining in full control, focusing only on her pleasure. But he should've known better than to believe Syndicorp tech might actually work in his favor. He bared his teeth at a long-limbed rakwiji bouncer standing in the path ahead, her scales flared in aggression. She grimaced back, long teeth glinting in the multi-colored lights, then seemed to think better of a confrontation and scurried out of the way.

He burst from the dark casino onto the brightly-lit sidewalk outside. Ignoring the outraged looks of other patrons, he shoved to the front of a line waiting for rickshaws and set Lisa in the back of the nearest one. When the human who'd been haggling price with the driver began to argue, Qaiyaan shoved him out of the way. The human skittered backward and fell onto his backside, his companions shouting in outrage. Qaiyaan didn't give an *anaq*. As he climbed in next to Lisa, he shouted at the driver, "Spaceport. Now. I'll pay double if you can get us there in under fifteen."

The driver lunged against the pedals, pulling the vehicle away from the curb and into the line of traffic. Picking up speed, the rickshaw careened past an oncoming u-bus, taking the corner toward the space station at breakneck speed.

Qaiyaan tapped his cochlear implant. "I'm on my way."

Mek's voice entered his head. "I told you to stay put."

"I'm not standing by helpless while you get your limp *ucuk* in gear. Where can we meet?"

A sigh. "The cargo doors. Any improvement?"

Qaiyaan pulled Lisa's torn dress closed over her breasts, wishing he could see into her brain. "No."

"You're sure you didn't nudge her?"

His previous pride about keeping control tasted like ashes. Had he nudged her? He'd been so into her, so tranced by her amazing body, that he wasn't sure. He didn't think he had. He hadn't felt a need to. The connection was already there, already calling him, telling him what she liked, what she needed. A presence that was uniquely Lisa. And she'd never told him to stop. Never warned him she was losing control. Her orgasm had washed deliciously over him, a moment of shared pleasure like he'd never felt before. His cock had been ready. Then the intangible bond had snapped. Twanged with a resonance that still rang through his blood-stream. He provided Mek the only answer he could. "She wanted to experiment. To see how far we could go."

The silence over his implant expressed Mek's disapproval far better than his words. "What the fuck were you thinking?"

Guilt clogged Qaiyaan's throat. Instead of answering, he tapped his implant to silence it then shouted at the driver, "Can't you go any faster?"

His entire crew was waiting at the open cargo bay doors when the rickshaw skidded to a halt on the blistering-hot tarmac. Qaiyaan lifted Lisa from the seat and strode toward the ship. Behind him, the driver clambered after him, cursing loudly for his promised fare. Shouting at his first mate to pay the angry yanipa-nimayu, Qaiyaan headed for the med bay. Mek ran alongside waving a portable scanner over Lisa's limp form.

Normally in an emergency situation, Qaiyaan would've sent a surge of ionic energy to his feet, allowing him to leap onto the second-level catwalk toward the med bay. But his terror of using any of his powers around the fragile woman in his arms sent him climbing the stairs three at a time.

In the med bay, he lay her gently on the exam table, pulling her gaping dress closed against his crewmen's gazes. When he felt Mek's hand on his arm, urging him away, he stiffened, instinct demanding he defend his woman. Then Mek's voice brought him back to reality. "I'm not sure what's causing her blackouts, but you're the common denominator. You need to leave."

Nausea rolled through him. He was the common denominator. Great *Ellam Cua*, what if he'd killed his only chance for a mate? He stepped backward, his attention glued to the woman on the table. To his *mate* on the table. Consummated or not, there was no denying that now. "She was trying to reprogram her own nanites. Trying to make us compatible."

Mek narrowed his eyes. "Was she successful?"

"Obviously not." Qaiyaan croaked out, his chest full of regret. Why had he ever allowed her to talk him into this?

Tovik moved between Qaiyaan and the exam table, his green eyes full of compassion. "Come on, Captain. I know where you hide the akluilak wine. Let the doctor do his thing."

Reluctantly, he followed his engineer to the galley.

Three shots of wine later, Qaiyaan felt no calmer. His soul felt like it'd been ripped in two. Tovik had been called away to talk to Nupnup's repairman, and Noatak now sat in the galley in silence, both feet propped on the neighboring chair, arms crossed over his chest. They both watched the door, waiting for Mek to make a report.

When the doctor arrived, he paused, face downturned as he read his handheld. Qaiyaan wanted to strangle him for taking so long yet was hesitant to interrupt the doctor's analysis. Noatak broke the silence. "Stop being an ass, Mek. If you're not ready to talk, go back to the med bay. The captain here's about to go into a rasvrid leviathan rage on our galley furniture."

Mek continued staring at his handheld. "Her brain waves are way off kilter, but it's different than last time. The nanites are reproducing and reprogramming at a rate I can't track. Her synapses can't keep up and I don't know how to stop it. She's so sensitive to energy frequencies, I can't get decent readings with my low-level sensors and I'm afraid anything more intense might make things worse. I've given her a test dose of a synaptic equalizer, but I'm not sure how human physiology will react." He lowered the device. "Can you tell me exactly what happened? Start at the very beginning, from the moment you left the spaceport."

Qaiyaan rose, scrubbing both hands over his face and up through his hair. He relayed every move they'd made, sanitizing their intimacy yet making it clear they'd taken that step. "But I didn't nudge her, I swear. I went no farther with her than any of us have with women during shore leave."

"I warned you that any intimacy could be too much for her." Mek's recriminating gaze barely touched Qaiyaan through his own quagmire of guilt.

"I know." Qaiyaan grabbed the wine and took a long swig directly from the bottle.

Tovik arrived, gaze sweeping from Mek to Qaiyaan. "The hull guy's almost done scanning the damaged panels. What'd I miss?"

Noatak kicked his feet off his makeshift footstool and reached for the bottle. "Mek just made the captain kiss and tell."

"Aw, man!"

"Shut up, you two," Mek warned.

Qaiyaan paced the small galley. The helplessness and rage he felt now were nearly as strong as what he'd felt upon hearing about the destruction of his planet and everyone he loved. "This is all my fault."

Mek once again consulted his handheld. "I wish I understood her nanite programming. It's made her more sensitive to a nudge than even perhaps a Denaidan female would be."

Tovik sat next to Noatak. "Or she just doesn't know how to shut the sensitivity off. Isn't that why our women couldn't leave the planet? They couldn't shut out the other races' input?"

Qaiyaan planted both hands on the table. "If she can't shut them off, can we remove them? Purify her blood or whatever?"

Mek's brows drew together. "I'm afraid it's not that simple. They've become so enmeshed with her synapses, removing them may do more harm than good."

An image of Lisa's mind overrun with tiny fucking robots filled Qaiyaan's mind. Robots she could never shut down. "She's still sensing me, isn't she? That's the problem."

"Perhaps. But she should avoid using her nanites until we figure this out."

"*She's* sensing him? Or those Syndicorp nanites are?" Noatak asked. "What if she's transmitting all this straight back to Syndicorp spies? I say we stick her back in cryo."

Mek nodded thoughtfully.

Qaiyaan put his hands on his hips and faced his crew. "We're not sticking her in cryo."

"Don't be so hasty. The idea may have merit." Mek was scrolling his handheld, gaze darting over the information as if he couldn't read it all fast enough.

"She's not a threat to us, not like that." Qaiyaan insisted. "And she nearly died in cryo last time."

"It's not that we don't trust her—" Mek started.

"*I* don't trust her," Noatak said.

Mek frowned at the first mate. "You're not helping." He turned back to Qaiyaan. "Slowing her nanites might break the programming cascade and allow her mind time to regain control. Plus we still haven't addressed the issue of her withstanding burn frequencies once we leave Bolisare. Cryo would stabilize her until we figure something out."

Qaiyaan took a deep breath, trying to remain rational. Much as he hated to admit it, Mek might be right. "So where do we get a cryo-pod?"

Tovik drummed his fingers on the table. "I made repairs to her old one. It should work even better now."

Noatak raised an eyebrow. "No offense, Tovik, but I'm not sure we should put her in one of your new and improved inventions."

Qaiyaan nodded. Tovik's most recent improvement to the *Hardship's* lavatory shower had used up half their water supply before they realized what was happening.

"Hey!" Tovik glowered at all three of his crewmen. "My upgrades have saved our asses more times than you can count."

"And I appreciate it when things work, Tovik. I really do. But this isn't the three of us going balls out to escape some heist. This is…" Qaiyaan wasn't sure how to explain. "This is Lisa. I'll go back to Nupnup and ask for a pod."

An unfamiliar voice spoke from behind him. "Too late for that."

Qaiyaan spun, hands balled into fists. A human male wearing a repairman's jumpsuit blocked the doorway, aiming a fully-charged pulse pistol straight between Qaiyaan's eyes.

CHAPTER ELEVEN

Lisa felt Qaiyaan's turmoil, a tug that reached deep into her soul and pleaded with her to pull free. The maelstrom surrounding her refused to let her go or even give her a chance to find solid ground within her own mind. Around the edges, she was also aware of the crew scrambling for options. Sweet Tovik's adoring concern. Mek's analytical worry. Even Noatak's grudging and conflicted wish to help her, in spite of his reluctance to hope. None of these connections could pull her free.

Then her cyber-sensitive nanites picked up an encoded message. They snatched bits out of the turmoil, piecing the packets of information together. There was a stranger on the ship. A cartel intruder.

And there were more on the way.

Adrenaline flooded her system, honing her focus. She had to warn the crew. The men who'd risked so much to save her were going to suffer and die. The cartel would punish them for helping her. Torture them as much for fun as retribution. The memory of a rakwiji bounty hunter using its claw to trace a bloody cartel tattoo over Seloh's chest slammed into her. She had to wake up. Now.

The nanites she'd reprogrammed continued to battle against those locked into Syndicorp protocols. Synapses in her brain fired at random, creating an ever-changing maze she couldn't escape. *You hacked the systems once. You can do it again.* She grabbed hold of one nanite. Just one. It took all the strength she had. But she gave it a single directive.

Wake me up.

The tiny computer burrowed its way through the electronic storm of her mind, dragging her behind like a kite. She bobbed to the surface of consciousness, sucking in a breath as if she'd been underwater. Her eyes flew open, blinded by the soft fluorescent lighting of the medical bay. She was alone in the room. After a couple of breaths to gather her strength, she attempted to sit, but her body refused to obey. *Come on, move!*

One finger at a time, one hand, one arm. She pushed herself upright. Using the nanite that'd brought her awake, she began reprogramming the others. But Syndicorp's programming was fighting back. Her forces were eroding. Instinct told her to shut everything down, initiate a reboot. But that would probably knock her out again, and she wasn't sure she'd ever wake up if that happened. All she could do was create a wall between her consciousness and her cyber-sensitivity to keep the Syndicorp faction at bay.

She swung her legs to the floor, her knees threatening to buckle. Her dress was held together across her chest with strips of medical tape, and an IV line trailed to her arm. She yanked the needle out and planted unsteady palms on the bed for support while she surveyed the med bay for a weapon. Anything to fend off the cartel infiltrator. She had no idea how he was here, or if the crew even knew about him yet. All she knew was he was waiting for reinforcements. Her hand fell on a pair of scissors, the only remotely aggressive thing in the bay unless she intended to bash him with a scanner. Threading her fingers through the loops, she crept out of the medical bay.

Down the hall, she heard Qaiyaan's outraged voice. "Who the fuck are you?"

A stranger dressed in workman's coveralls had his back to her, bracing himself with one foot in and one foot outside the galley door.

"That's the hull repairman," Tovik said from inside the room.

The man gestured to someone inside. "Pick up the rope and tie your friend, there. You guys made a serious mistake trying to put one over on the cartel."

Lisa ducked across the corridor into Qaiyaan's quarters and peeked around the doorframe. The galley was two doors down, only about fifteen steps away, but her legs felt weak as jelly. She caught her breath and fought to keep her nanites under control.

"There must be some sort of mistake," Qaiyaan said. "I want to talk to Nupnup."

"Oh, you'll be talking to Nupnup, all right. You can explain to him how you're charging services to one of the cells Syndicorp took out of commission six months ago."

Lisa's stomach dropped. Of course cell three had been destroyed. That cell had been the point of entry she and Doug had provided when they'd signed on with Syndicorp. How stupid could she be? The code words hadn't been changed because they were obsolete. Now Qaiyaan was in danger because of her mistake.

"Taken out? How the fuck did that happen?" Qaiyaan asked. "We've been in deep cover."

Good explanation, Lisa thought to herself and slid out of the room, creeping toward the stranger. *Keep him talking.*

Lisa?

Qaiyaan's voice in her head sent her to her knees. The scissors went clattering across the metal deck. Stars swam in her vision and she struggled to stay conscious, ordering the few nanites she controlled to subdue her misfiring synapses. She was barely aware of the sound of a struggle, of the zipping noise of a pulse gun, shouting and cursing. She had to help them, but her control of her body was sluggish as if the nanites were trying to take over her motor skills now, too.

Feet pounded the decking nearby, and hands cradled both sides of her face. She blinked up into Qaiyaan's blue eyes.

"Lisa! Thank *Ellam Cua* you're alive!" he breathed.

Her nanites swarmed toward his touch as if yearning for the contact of his copper skin. But that meant the few she controlled weren't keeping her synapses in line, either. She jerked away, breath coming in painful gasps. "We have to lift off planet. Now."

"I'm all for getting off this hell-hole." Noatak had a knee planted firmly on the cartel member's back, keeping the guy pinned against the deck. Waves of anger emanated from both men, smashing against her nanite-battered synapses and making her want to curl into a ball.

The stranger struggled, his gaze settling on Lisa. "Lisa Moss?" His eyes narrowed. "The Syndicorp spy. Gedan Jaru will pay big bucks for proof you're alive."

One of his brown eyes went opaque white then dark again. *Shit.* He had a cybernetic camera. Did he have a transmission unit, too? She couldn't tell without using her nanites, but wasn't sure she could keep her synapses under control if she did. The little computers were going crazy as if picking up every nearby emotion. The tumult in her head was making it hard to think. "He has a camera in his left eye."

Qaiyaan grabbed the stranger by the hair. "Someone get me a knife."

"What are you doing?" Mek asked.

"Removing his camera."

"He's probably already sent his intel." Mek held out a warning hand. "Cutting it out won't do any good."

"It'll make me feel better," Qaiyaan growled. The protective urges rolling off the big captain might've seemed sexy if Lisa hadn't been so overwhelmed with the emotions pressing in from all around her.

Noatak wrenched the stranger's arm backward at an awkward angle. "He mentioned Syndicorp spies. He could have useful info."

"*Anaq!*" Qaiyaan swore and released his hold.

The stranger bared his teeth, but kept his gaze on Lisa. "I have lots of intel. What's it worth to you?"

Lisa held her body stiff as stone, fighting off the oily waves of greed coming from the stranger. But she also sensed a wobble in his emotions. A hesitation that could only mean one thing.

The stranger was stalling, waiting for an opportunity to send the photo to Gedan.

She stared at him, her eyes burning as she realized what that meant. *He doesn't have a transmission unit.* She could delete the picture.

Rising, she wobbled over to the man, dropping to her knees beside him. "I'm going to hack into his camera and erase the picture."

Noatak grabbed both her wrists stopping her before she made contact. "So you can wipe what he knows about you? I don't think so."

She glowered and jerked away. "I can't reprogram his brain, only his camera."

"How do we know that?"

Lisa balled her hands into fists until her nails cut into her palms, using the pain as a focus. "You don't. But if word gets out I'm alive, every cartel contact in the galaxy will be after our blood."

Freed from Noatak's arm-wrenching, the stranger propped himself on his elbows, craning his neck to look behind him. "I have a proposition. How about we split the money? She's pretty. We can have some fun with her, then turn her in."

In an instant, Qaiyaan yanked the stranger out from under Noatak and slammed a fist against his cheekbone. With a satisfying crunch, the stranger rocked backward, colliding with the wall before sliding down it in a daze. Qaiyaan loomed over him like a pillar of rage. "How about you shut the fuck up."

Grimacing, Noatak pointed at Lisa. "If the cartel wants her this bad, maybe we should give her to them. Making a little cash sounds a hell of a lot better than adding to our list of enemies."

"You want some of this, too, Noatak?" Muscles coiled and hands balled into fists, Qaiyaan stepped toward his first mate.

But Lisa knew Noatak was partially right. The cartel would never stop coming after her. Anyone associated with her was doomed. Qaiyaan deserved better. The crew of the *Hardship* deserved better. Taking a deep breath, she said, "If the cartel finds out you helped me, you'll never be safe again. I won't let that happen. Leave me behind."

Qaiyaan scowled and clenched his hands at his sides. "We don't abandon crew members."

Tovik gestured down the hall with his pulse pistol. "We can't leave you. They'll find you for sure."

"I spent most of my life on Whylon Station hiding from one cartel goon or another." She nodded toward the stranger. "Destroy the camera. And when you're done questioning him, it's probably best if he dies." She hated to think like the cartel, but she saw no other way.

Pushing to her feet, she ran through potential contacts here on Bolisare. She'd have to start at ground zero, picking pockets and living on the street like she had on Whylon. Only on Whylon, she hadn't had a bounty on her head. Plus she'd had Doug at her side. How was she going to find him without help? Her vision swam in and out of focus, and she directed all the energy she had into fortifying the walls her nanites had built. She had to stay upright long enough to get off the ship and find a place to hide. Then she'd think about finding Doug.

As if he could read her thoughts, Qaiyaan said, "I promised to find your brother."

She swallowed and took a step toward the cargo bay. "You already rescued me once. For that I thank you. But I don't need your help."

Qaiyaan crossed his arms, widening his stance to block the narrow corridor. "I'm not leaving you."

All this arguing made it feel like she was standing on a two-g planet. Fierce protectiveness swelled off Qaiyaan in waves, burying Tovik and Mek's concern, and even consuming the stranger's oily greed. Only Noatak's distrust, filling the air around her like a windstorm, pounded against her with an equal force.

Lisa scowled at the first mate. "I'm leaving, Noatak, so stop bombarding me with your doubts. I can barely keep my brain from exploding from Qaiyaan's feelings as it is."

The tension in the room faltered. What could only be described as a curtain dropped between her and the chaos, muting the gale force without completely silencing it. The sudden break from emotional pressure was such a relief she wanted to cry.

Noatak squared himself to face her, his face blank. "You can sense my emotions?"

Lisa nodded.

"Can you sense mine?" Tovik asked.

She smiled weakly. "I think I'd be able to feel yours even without nanites."

"Try to talk to her, Qaiyaan!" the young man said.

Lisa closed her eyes against the renewed pressure of Tovik's excitement. "Tovik, can you scale it back, please?"

"Sorry." The flickering emotion dropped.

Noatak curled his upper lip, but Lisa could sense the hope behind his disgust. "How can a human sense us? She only has one heart."

Uncertainty hung like a cloud around Qaiyaan. "I thought I heard her talking in my head earlier."

Lisa met his gaze, her heartbeat fluttering as she remembered the touch of his mind. "You heard me? I thought I heard you, too. That's what made me trip in the hallway."

Mek scratched his stubbled jaw. "The nanites might be creating a synaptic flow without the aid of a secondary heart. I'd like to try some medication and see if she stabilizes."

"In case you've forgotten, the cartel will be here any moment." Noatak jammed a knee into the stranger's kidneys and began tying his hands behind his back. "We don't have time for science experiments."

Startled back to the moment, Lisa regarded the stranger and licked her lips. "I still think you'd be safer without me."

"If you think we're letting you go now, you're crazy," Tovik grinned at her. "What I wouldn't give for a woman I could link with."

"Tovik, hush." Turning to Lisa, Qaiyaan sighed. His electric blue eyes sought hers. "Please let Mek do those tests. He may be the only doc in the galaxy who knows how to help you. And us."

She swayed from the tangible power emanating from the captain's powerful frame. She wanted to accept. To stay and make him hers. But if the cartel caught them, it would be Seloh all over again. She couldn't bear to see Qaiyaan tortured to death like that.

Qaiyaan stepped close and lowered his head until his breath caressed her skin. "I need you to stay with me. Please?"

She raised her eyes to his, biting her lip. If anyone could hold their own against the cartel, Qaiyaan could. And she needed him. Not just to find Doug, or fix her nanites. She needed his strength. His presence by her side. Taking a deep breath, she nodded. "All right."

CHAPTER TWELVE

Qaiyaan watched Lisa depart to the med bay, her gaze lingering on his until she disappeared around the corner, then turned his attention back to the stranger. "Sure would be handy to have a brig right now, wouldn't it?"

"We should just push him out the back during liftoff." Noatak tightened the rope holding the man's wrists behind his back. "No telling what other cybernetic gizmos he's got on him that might sabotage us."

"We could stick him in the cryo-pod," Tovik said.

"Not a bad idea." Qaiyaan grabbed the stranger by the collar and hoisted him to his feet.

"You were just saying the cryo-pod wasn't working!" the man choked out, struggling feebly against Qaiyaan's grip.

"Would you rather be pushed out the airlock?" Qaiyaan started pushing him toward the cargo bay. "Noatak, get us airborne. Tovik, with me."

After stuffing the struggling and cursing man into the pod and slamming the lid closed, Qaiyaan watched Tovik fiddle with the controls. The man's muffled shouts could be heard through the pod's thick lid, his breath clouding the small window. The light inside alternated from amber to red and back again. Qaiyaan asked, "You sure you don't need Mek?"

"Nah, I got the basics." The light settled on amber, then flashed green. Tovik stood, brushing his hands together in satisfaction. "See?"

"All right." A surge of extra gravity set the deck thrumming. *Liftoff.* So much for getting the *Hardship's* outer plating fixed before they had to endure another burn. *Ellam Cua, let it hold together.* He and his men could withstand void if the ship popped a seam, but he had a new crew member to consider. What were they going to do with her when it was time to burn? They still hadn't resolved her nanite's sensitivity to burn frequencies.

Tovik headed for the engine room, while Qaiyaan took the catwalk stairs two at a time. He reached the small control room in time to see the pale blue lower atmosphere transition to violet and then black outside the view screen. Mek stood hunched next to Noatak, who leaned over the dashboard from the nav seat. Lisa sat buckled in the captain's chair, her eyes squeezed closed. Someone had given her a loose shirt to wear over the bodice of her dress, but a long, sexy slice of leg still peeked from the side slit.

Noatak's fingers darted over the command surface, guiding the ship to avoid incoming traffic. "Air control isn't happy with us right now."

Qaiyaan couldn't read the screens from his position at the door, and there were already too many bodies in the cramped space. "How long until we clear the buffer?"

"Sixteen or seventeen minutes, assuming I can avoid any orbiting cartel." Noatak tapped an adjustment into his controls as a spiny garan'uk pleasure vehicle slid past the view screen. "You have a destination in mind?"

"Any place but here."

"If we find my brother," Lisa's voice could barely be heard over the engines. "He can reprogram my nanites."

Qaiyaan put a hand on the door frame to steady himself as the ship rocked under Noatak's guidance. "Let's tackle one thing at a time, okay? We need to clear air control."

The deck shuddered, and Noatak made another adjustment to his controls. "We've got a tail."

"*Anaq*," Qaiyaan swore. A tail already? He squinted at the viewscreen, unable to tell friend from foe among the scattered couriers and cargo vessels coming and going from the surface. But Noatak had done this often enough, Qaiyaan trusted he was right. "Can we slingshot off the atmosphere straight to burn?"

"Lisa can't take the stress unshielded," Mek said.

Qaiyaan leveled him with a gaze. "I'm fully aware of that. We'll have to stabilize her like we did last time."

Mek said, "You can't—"

"Don't lecture me about over-using recovery stims," Qaiyaan interrupted, acutely aware of Noatak's addiction to the drug. Everyone generally tread carefully around the subject with him. "We don't have time to argue. We can do this."

"*We* probably can." Mek pointed between himself and Tovik. "*You* can't. You send her into a coma when you touch her."

Air suddenly refused to enter Qaiyaan's lungs. How could he have forgotten that? *Because you don't want it to be true.* He met Lisa's gaze. Her eyes had the same glazed look he remembered his sister having after her empathic suppression classes. "Can the two of you stabilize her?"

Mek glanced at Tovik and shook his head. "Not alone."

Qaiyaan swallowed and faced Noatak, who remained facing the controls. His friend had been with him long before the planet's destruction and was as close to Qaiyaan as a brother. They'd enlisted together and served on the same task force with the troopers. They'd grieved together at the loss of their world. And Qaiyaan had been at Noatak's side every moment his friend had struggled to overcome his stim addiction. But he needed to help Lisa. *They* needed to help Lisa. She held the key to their future, Noatak's included.

Before Qaiyaan could even form the words to ask, though, Noatak swiveled in his seat. "Take the helm. And watch your six for that tail."

"*Iluq*, are you sure?" If Qaiyaan'd ever felt guilt in his life, it was nothing compared to this moment.

Noatak's voice remained calm and quiet. "We don't leave crew behind."

Chest tight, Qaiyaan spared a final glance at Lisa as he slid into the nav seat. He wasn't nearly as good a pilot as Noatak, but he'd get them out of here.

From the door, Mek said, "Give a shout when you're ready to burn."

"Keep her safe," Qaiyaan called back. But Mek and Lisa were already down the corridor. He felt their departure like a void.

Qaiyaan banked the *Hardship* starboard as he cleared Bolisare's atmosphere. They'd been strafed by at least one laser blast during their escape, adding to the hull's numerous scars, but he'd lost their tail by weaving between the thick stream of traffic coming in and out of the station. Luckily, the cartel didn't appear to have a ship waiting in orbit, and Qaiyaan skimmed the planet's gravitational pull while picking up speed. He planned to slingshot off the nearby moon—a highly illegal move in most populated systems—but this was Bolisare, not some Syndicorp-governed speed bump. He intended to use every advantage to get them as far away as possible.

He programmed the burn drive to aim for the Milicon quadrant, a parsec away from Alleigh. His constant tracking of Syndicorp CEOs and shipping activity gave him the gut feeling that the lab Lisa was looking for might be at that particular edge of Syndicorp space. While the burn drive pulled at every molecule of his being, he gripped the arms of the nav chair and stared at the holocube Noatak kept on the dashboard, the image of his parents a constant reminder of what Syndicorp had destroyed. A constant reminder of their mission as pirates. Stealing Lisa's brother from Syndicorp's clutches was going to be satisfying on so many levels.

The burn itself only took a handful of seconds, but it always felt like the event lasted hours. When the galaxy finally realigned itself, Qaiyaan checked his sensors for nearby ships. Unless a ship had been in his immediate wake and prepped for burn, he couldn't have been followed. But he hadn't lived this long by not being careful. Scanners showed nothing but empty space. Good. He needed to check on Lisa and the rest of his crew. Lifting himself on unsteady legs, he stumbled out of the control room airlock and down the stairs to the med bay.

Lisa was sitting up on the medical table, forehead pressed against her bent knees. Qaiyaan took a deep breath of relief. "Thank *Ellam Cua* you're all right."

She let out a shaky gasp in response, as if unable to summon anything more.

He wanted—needed—to pull her against him, to feel her heartbeat against his. To reassure himself she was indeed alive and whole. But touching her would definitely not accomplish that. A bone-deep sorrow filled him, knowing that his deepest desire might forever remain out of his reach. Instead, he knelt next to Tovik, who was slumped on the floor against the medical bay cot. Mek and Noatak were similarly sprawled around the bed. They must've all stood around her for the burn, holding her and then collapsing with exhaustion afterward.

Qaiyaan reached out to find Tovik's pulse. Alive but unconscious. He rose and checked the other two, then stepped over the doctor's body, opening the cabinet where they kept the recovery stims. Priming the stim gun with a dose, he administered it to Mek.

The doctor stiffened, eyelids flying open and pupils constricted to pinpricks. He sat up unsteadily, his voice thick and languid, but coherent. "The others?"

"I wanted you up and running first." Qaiyaan primed the stim gun with a second dose.

Mek nodded. "Noatak wants to recover on his own. I'll see to him. You handle Tovik."

A lump filled Qaiyaan's throat, and he moved to the young man. Much like Mek, Tovik awakened with a start, eyes wild. But he also had a grin on his face. "Whoa." He twisted and pulled himself upright to peer at Lisa over the edge of her bed. "Wild ride, but we did it."

Lisa looked out of the corner of her eye at the young man, a tiny smile tweaking the corner of her mouth.

Tovik's enthusiasm was infectious as always, but Qaiyaan's thoughts remained heavy. Mek was arranging a limp Noatak on the second med cot. The energy required to hold one's self through burn was bearable. For some reason using it to hold another person steady was exponentially more exhausting. Noatak would take days to bounce back without the aid of stims.

Adjusting the gown around her legs, Lisa swung her legs over the edge of the bed, her attention also on the doctor's activity. "Will Noatak be all right?"

Mek's lips remained tight.

An inkling of fear settled in Qaiyaan's hearts. "Will he?" He searched for Noatak's ionic signature. His first mate's hearts beat slowly, nearly undetectable, but steady. "Thank *Ellam Cua*."

The doctor turned to gather supplies from the cupboards. His hands were shaking, full of erratic, stim-induced energy. "Give him some time."

Lisa stood, her bare feet making no sound on the floor, and moved to Noatak's side. The fingers of one hand fluttered over her mouth. "This is because of me. God, what if he dies?" She looked up at Qaiyaan. "You shouldn't have let him do this."

Noatak's voice creaked from the cot. "I'm not dead."

An exclamation of surprise escaped Lisa, and she leaned down to press her cheek to Noatak's.

Tovik, still sitting on the floor, let out what could only be called a giggle, his fingers waggling in response to whatever stim-inspired ideas were swimming through his head. "Noatak's too bad-tempered to die."

Qaiyaan turned to shove the stim gun back into its cabinet. He longed for Lisa's touch, her cheek against his. The sensation of her voice in his head earlier could only mean one thing—she was his mate. Their resonances aligned. Yet in spite of the connection, in spite of his conviction that she was the one, he'd never be able to touch her. Never be able to truly make her his own.

The overhead lights flickered as if in response to his thoughts, and the hull groaned. *Anaq, what else can go wrong?* Qaiyaan spun and stepped over Tovik toward the door. "I should check our system. No telling what that guy in our cryo-pod did to the ship before this all started."

Noatak pushed Lisa away and tried to sit up. "I'll help."

Mek placed one palm flat against the prone man's chest. "Don't try to move. I need to check your secondary heart."

"What's wrong with his heart?" Qaiyaan paused halfway across the small bay.

The doctor and Noatak exchanged a glance. "It's nothing, captain," Noatak said. "Just let the doc do his job. You concentrate on finding this mystical magical brother who can fix Lisa's nanites. I can't hold her steady every time we engage the burn drive."

Lisa snuck in one last flutter of her fingertips over Noatak's brow. "Thank you again."

He scowled and rolled his eyes, which was about as much of a "you're welcome" as Noatak ever gave anyone.

Noatak grunted, ignoring the doctor's orders, and sat up. His copper skin seemed abnormally dark, its satiny gleam dulled by a greenish cast. "I can get started looking for that secret lab. Where'd you eject us, Captain?"

"Milicon sector. Captain Kashatok's been working the shipping lanes here since the Termination. He might know something."

Mek let his scanner fall to his side and glared at Qaiyaan. "You're going to trust that drunken excuse for a Denaidan?"

"He knows the sector," Qaiyaan insisted in spite of the nausea riding low in his belly. Kashatok ran one of the seedier crews among the Denaidan pirates, but he was also the only actual cartel member among the fleet and a source of valuable intel.

"I can hack into the darkweb," Lisa said. "I'm sure I still have contacts who—"

"No." Noatak and Mek said simultaneously.

Tovik dragged himself onto the mattress like a nerelian ice slug. "You can access the dark web?" His words were slurred. "Can you track down the schematic for a pynergic quark converter there?"

"We have more pressing concerns, Tovik." Qaiyaan tried to glare, but concern for his engineer weighed heavy on his already guilty-as-hell conscience. Two stim doses this close together could cause serious damage.

Mek sighed and plodded over with a scanner. "I'd better sedate him. Hold still, Tovik."

Qaiyaan turned to Lisa. "The darkweb's too dangerous. We have to assume your contacts have been compromised." The lights browned out and flickered back up again, accompanied by a throaty vibration through the deck plating.

"I should check the hull." Noatak attempted to rise but ended up flopping back down on the cot.

"I told you to stay put," Mek said, leaning heavily on the edge of Tovik's cot.

"You should rest, too." Lisa pushed the chair from the nearby computer toward him.

"A doctor's job is never done." Yet Mek's big frame collapsed onto the chair, bending forward to rest his head on the edge of the mattress next to Tovik.

Qaiyaan took a deep breath. Between Tovik and Noatak, Mek had his hands full. Yet the hull needed checking, which meant someone had to go outside. A diagnostic needed to be run to make sure the electrical system wasn't going to short out life-support. He had a prisoner in the cargo bay who should be looked in on. Everything fell on Qaiyaan's shoulders.

"You have an extra crew member now." Lisa moved to within arm's length, sexy as hell in that loose shirt over her gold, form-fitting dress, her charcoal hair in an alluring disarray.

"You know how to run a ship diagnostic?"

She raised an eyebrow and tapped her temple. "I'm pretty sure we can figure it out."

Mek sat up woozily. "The synaptic equalizer I gave her could wear off unexpectedly. She should avoid using her nanites. Let me do it."

Lisa crossed her arms. "I can run auto-checks without using my nanites. You need to stay here." She moved to the door before anyone could deny her. "Besides, I know computer systems far better than I understand alien physiology."

Qaiyaan couldn't help checking out her perfectly rounded ass until she disappeared around the corner. If it took him the rest of his life, he'd look for a way to be together, starting with finding her brother. He snapped out of his lustful thoughts and dodged through the doorway after her. "Seal the airlock behind you. I've got to void the ship so I can work on the hull. I'll be sealing off the cargo bay, but I'd prefer you behind double airlocks. I'll let you know when it's safe again."

"Be careful, okay? I'm not talented enough to make this ship chase you if you go floating off into space."

He chuckled and reached for her, intending to give her a kiss, then caught himself. They exchanged an awkward glance, then turned their separate ways.

CHAPTER THIRTEEN

L isa sealed the airlock and settled into the captain's chair, pulling up the ship diagnostics. The injection Mek'd given her just before burn had eased the chaos in her head. She knew the nanites were still warring, but her synapses no longer fired in response to the attacks. The doctor had explained how it all worked; something about human synapses being promiscuous and hooking up in new ways? The biology was way over her head, so she'd just nodded and been grateful for the relief, however temporary he warned her it could be.

On the dashboard, she slid aside a holocube displaying the 3D image of a much younger Noatak wearing an innocent smile sitting next to a man and a woman. His parents? She'd have to take a closer look later. Right now, she needed to figure out this ship's systems. The control panel lit up with several segments of data at her touch. During her time in the corp' lab, she'd practiced hacking ship systems, but it had never been intuitive for her. She could recognize basic sequences without the aid of her nanites, so she looked for the code controlling life-support.

Every vessel's interface was slightly different, and after setting life-support's auto-diagnostic, she noted the ship had an internal camera system. After a few minutes of fumbling, she engaged the one in the cargo bay. An image came on-screen just in time to show Qaiyaan venting the bay door, the barest hint of a shimmer around his body. He'd explained that he could endure the vacuum of space for ten or twenty minutes—even longer if he didn't exert himself. She bit her lip, sure he was about to be sucked out of reach. But his feet remained locked to the floor, his long hair and beard pulled outward in the escaping air.

As if sensing her watching him, he looked over his shoulder at the camera and nodded once. His cochlear implant would allow her to speak to him through the comm, but he couldn't respond in the vacuum. His flowing hair relaxed into a billowing halo at the same moment her stomach fell out from under her; the gravity system had dropped. *Whoa.* He hadn't mentioned losing gravity. Her ass lifted off the captain's seat, and she put a hand up to keep from bumping her head on the ceiling.

Luckily, the control room was small, and she grappled for the safety straps on the chair. The ship shuddered while the big bay doors cranked the rest of the way open. Qaiyaan took a few slow steps down the cargo ramp. His broad shoulders cut angular lines across the velvet blackness of space beyond. As if he wore a full vacuum-worker's suit, he walked around the edge and disappeared.

She checked the scrolling diagnostics again. Several blinking red lines indicated issues, but they'd already been flagged at some point by the crew and obviously pushed aside until later. She was looking for something new. One of the panels chirped at her, and she scanned the surface of the dash for the source. The proximity sensor. Probably Qaiyaan walking around on the ship. She returned to the diagnostic. The ship shuddered, rocking her in her seat harness. Frowning, she looked at the cargo bay camera again and gasped. The dull, black patina of a cartel courier ship sat parked in the bay.

"Qaiyaan!" She scrambled toward the comm. "There's a cartel ship in our cargo bay!" Where had it come from? Had they seen him?

The small black ship's doors winged open, disgorging two rakwiji in vacuum helms packing military-grade pulse pistols. Their hard, scaly hides allowed their bodies to withstand vacuum as well as a suit. Bile rose in her throat. "Two rakwiji with pistols."

She didn't even know if Qaiyaan could hear her. What if he hadn't seen them and came back to a trap? She had to do something. She looked around for a vacuum suit, but the control room was empty.

Qaiyaan's voice filled her head, solid as if he was standing right next to her. *Stay put. I'm coming.*

Her breath choked off at the sensation of him in her mind. Her nanites shot woozy sparks across her vision. Was Mek's shot wearing off?

One of the bounty hunters clumped to the bay door controls, magnetic grav-boots slowing his movements. It carried a disk the size of a man's footprint. At the control panel, it slapped the disk over the keyboard.

The doors began to close.

Her vision swelled and shrank in time to her thundering heartbeat. She keyed the comm again. "Hurry, Qaiyaan! The doors!"

Fingers flying over the controls, she tried to override whatever the invaders had done. Error messages popped up across every screen. ACCESS DENIED. They'd placed some kind of lock on it, probably that big disk. The doors sealed shut with a thump she could feel through the deck. Terror settled like a rock in her stomach. How long could Qaiyaan stay out there? "I can't override them!"

Warn the others. His voice floated into her mind again.

She engaged the comm to the med bay. "Mek, Noatak, Tovik, wake up!"

No response.

She pulled up a second screen with a view to the med bay. All three men lay sound asleep, strapped to the medical cots to keep them in place without gravity. Again, she keyed the comm. "We're being boarded! Wake up!"

The men didn't budge. She called Qaiyaan again. "I can't wake them up."

He didn't respond either.

She scanned the comm diagnostics. The comm wasn't transmitting. She'd been locked out. She couldn't warn the crew or Qaiyaan. She was all alone and rakwiji were on board. Her heart threatened to break through her ribcage. *Qaiyaan!*

Stop panicking. His mental voice was calm. Reassuring.

She took a deep breath, looking around as if he might appear next to her. *You can hear me?*

Yes. Now tell me what's happening.

Her nanites hummed at the edge of wakefulness, but she tamped them down. She wasn't sure how she was talking to Qaiyaan without them, but she knew in her gut she couldn't give them control. *They have the ship systems completely locked down; communications, navigation, even life support.*

There's another access portal near the thrusters. His thoughts sounded strained. *Can you open it?*

I'll try. Eager for a solution, she read through lines of code, looking for a way around the block the rakwiji had put on the systems. If only Doug was here. A block like this would be nothing more than an inconvenience for him, even before he'd received the nanites.

Full gravity returned with a jarring rush, pressing her into the seat cushions and slamming her arms against the control panel. She checked on the men in the med bay again, but they still hadn't budged. They must be even more exhausted than they'd let on. Either that or Mek'd given them something to help them rest. She wished she had sight of Qaiyaan, but she could no longer access the other cameras.

She continued trying to hack into the portal in engineering. Panic was making her brain jumpy. How would Doug look at this code? Maybe if she thought like him, she could find a way in.

The rakwiji crouched in feral positions, conversing next to their ship, their helms still in place. Although they'd engaged gravity, they'd elected not to reestablish atmosphere. They probably thought they had the crew at a disadvantage. The larger one pointed to a nearby cargo box, a sharp-toothed grin visible inside its faceplate. A familiar, blinking green light illuminated the viewport on what had been her cryo-pod.

The smaller rakwiji moved toward it, its mate scuttling close behind. The two exchanged leering gazes, and then the first rakwiji extended a necrotic claw, tracing the viewport. With slow, almost sensuous movements, it tapped a command into the pod's control panel. The second rakwiji rocked back and forth, scales rippling with excitement as the light in the pod flashed red.

The lid popped open, and Lisa could imagine the hiss of escaping air as the cartel guy half-fell from the box. He rolled onto his side, looking up at his rescuers with a horrible grimace. His face turned purple and his eyes bulged. One pleading hand extended toward them, but the rakwiji only stepped back and watched, toothy grins gleaming through their faceplates. Lisa couldn't look away, reminded of Seloh's torturous death at rakwiji hands. Is this what would happen to Qaiyaan when he could no longer keep up his shield? She wanted to vomit.

Jabbing at the control panels, Lisa tried to force the internal comm system to work. Tried to think like her brother. But her clumsy hacking attempts only covered her screens in error messages. She had to warn the crew. Make them get up. Get ready for battle. But they were all but helpless in the med bay.

With the cartel man dead, the rakwiji headed for the catwalk, side-by-side like the prey animals they were.

Qaiyaan, they just killed their own man. Silence roared in her ears. *Qaiyaan?*

I'm working on it. Qaiyaan's frustration pounded at her. His need to breathe couldn't be masked. He was running out of air.

She pictured his face, his beautiful copper skin darkening, his features disfiguring. Adrenaline had her hands trembling as her fingertips pounded the control panel with every hacker command she knew.

ACCESS DENIED.

Qaiyaan's voice reached her, faint along the mental connection. *I want you to know that I love you, Lisa.*

Every muscle in her body tingled. This was not how she wanted to hear his feelings. *Don't give up.*

She stared at the error boxes plastered across her screens. Her skills weren't good enough, not without help. There was only one thing to do. Squeezing her eyes shut, she placed her palms flat against the dashboard and gathered her nanites. Qaiyaan would die if she didn't get him inside. She needed to override the lockouts, to at least give him and the others a chance.

Packets of cyber-information threatened to knock her flat against the nav chair.

Don't. Qaiyaan's voice held command, even though she could sense he was failing. *I'll figure something out.*

There's no time. Savoring the last brush of his mind across hers, she said, *I love you, Qaiyaan.*

And dove into the ship's system.

Qaiyaan stared at the blackened streak across the *Hardship's* hull, his oxygen-deprived brain turning the laser damage into a monstrous grin under the beam of his headlamp. *Lisa?* She was no longer answering his thoughts. His heart beat too rapidly in his ears, burning precious oxygen at a rate he couldn't afford. *Anaq, Lisa, answer me!*

He grimaced at the damage and pounded a fist against the plating. His body lifted away, free-floating toward open space. Clamping his fingers around the edge of the nearby landing fin, he dragged himself back toward the ship. Maintaining his ionic connection was becoming more difficult.

Maybe you should just let go. If Lisa was gone, what did he have to live for, anyway? His crew was comatose, at the mercy of cartel bounty hunters who would probably chop up the *Hardship* for salvage—right after they chopped up the crew.

No. That was the oxygen deprivation talking. He'd die before he gave up.

Hand-over-hand, he pulled himself between the landing fins and paused at the sealed access door into engineering. The entry panel was dark and unresponsive. *Anaq.* He'd hoped Lisa would be successful. That some miracle might give him a fighting chance. Instead, the woman he loved was in trouble. *Lisa, wake up!*

He couldn't feel her in his mind like he had before. He panned the light of his headlamp along the hull again as if the dull metal surface might provide more options. His lungs burned with a desire for air. The cartel ship must've pulled into the *Hardship's* wake mere moments before the burn and somehow hidden here in a blind spot between the fins during his initial scans. Sneaky cartel bastards.

The comm webbing embedded across the hull was broken by laser fire in a couple of places. Tovik had connected an external booster to the comm array to act as an independent backup if they took too much damage. The chance of someone being within signal range was slim to none, but at the very least Qaiyaan wanted to leave a message. A legacy. The other Denaidans out there deserved to know how close he'd been to finding a mate. Mek's medical notes had to be worth something.

Edging along the ship's exterior, he reached the comm junction and had to pause to calm his breathing. The dire cold of space was leaching through his shield and sinking into his bones, making it hard to move. His fingers were stiff, but he managed to open the junction box. Inside, Tovik's booster keypad was affixed to the side wall. The micro-screen blazed to life at Qaiyaan's touch. Using the frequency the Denaidan fleet used to alert each other of Syndicorp activity, he entered the ship's coordinates then encoded the message:

Under attack by cartel. Medical breakthrough on board.

The message was so inadequate, he laughed, and the expulsion of air caused his oxygen shield to slip. Icy vacuum nipped at his skin before he re-established control. Fuck it, he thought, and typed in:

If you ever hope to have sex again, send help.

That ought to get the fleet's attention. Putting the broadcast on repeat, he headed back toward the access door to engineering. The message would continue to play until the booster's battery pack ran out. Maybe someone in this sector would stumble across it. Some-day. After he and Lisa were long gone.

Ahead of him, the door's keypad looked like it was glow-ing. His vision swam, stars pressing in around the edges of consciousness. His ribcage felt as if bands were tightening around his torso, keeping him from taking a full breath. Staying connected to the ship took every bit of his concentration. He reached the access door, every muscle quivering with cold and exhaustion.

The keypad was live.

Chapter Fourteen

L isa steeled herself and hacked at the blocking codes like she was wielding a machete. Each blow sent her reeling backward into darkness. Pulling herself out of the depths to renew her attack grew more and more difficult. She'd never been as good as Doug. Never would be, with or without the nanites. She wished for her brother, to know he was okay. Or at least tell him goodbye. *Doug, I'm sorry. I wanted to find you.*

Little Sis, is that you? The words froze her in place. They couldn't be real. Could they?

Doug?

Lisa? Are you here? Unlike Qaiyaan's rich, reverberant tones, this voice had a tinny quality, but it was Doug.

Thank God you're alive! She projected, her nanites thrumming like live wires. *Where are you?*

Syndicorp told me you were dead. His uncertainty reminded her of their years in the slums, each day a question of survival.

It's okay, Doug. Lisa reached through the connection for her twin, seeking to ground herself, to ground them both. The physical contact might not be there, but the mental one felt just as real. *The corp' didn't kill me, but the cartel is hot on my tail. We're under attack by bounty hunters and I can't remove the block on this ship's systems. My nanites aren't strong enough. Can you help fix them like you used to?*

Cartel? How did they find you?

Doug, there's no time to go into that. I need your help right now!

We're communicating faster than you realize. Doug's presence fluttered through her mind as if turning the pages of a book. *The mind can process thousands of gigabytes per second, and memories are just data, after all. Your ship must be acting like an antenna between our nanites.* In nanoseconds, he knew everything; Syndicorp's betrayal, Mek's work on her synapses, her newfound telepathy, and her growing love for a copper-skinned alien. In return, she sensed a series of bright lights and examination tables, advanced implants, escape attempts, and a heartbreaking sense of loss from her brother.

Doug, what have they done to you? This was her twin, the person she'd shared everything with since before birth. Yet he was somehow different. Something was really wrong.

Soon your body won't be your own anymore, Doug responded, heartbreak in his voice. *The nanites will take over. You'll be more machine than human. They're nearing critical system deployment already.*

Shock loosed her grip on him. *What are you saying?*

You need to get rid of them. The sooner the better. They're changing you, and once they engage their core protocols, you won't be able to live without them. Syndicorp will own you. As they do me.

No! Tell me where you are! Once we rescue you, we can come up with a plan to use our nanites against the corp'.

His presence slipped from her grasp like mist. *It's too dangerous. Don't look for me. Stay far away.*

Stop being overprotective. Qaiyaan and his crew have promised to help me. As soon as I wake up and get rid of these bounty hunters, we're coming to find you. She stretched out and grabbed hold of him, this time refusing to let go. *Have you tried to reprogram your own nanites? I've done it a little with mine, and you're way better at this stuff than I am.*

You think too much of me. His wry smile transferred through their connection as if she was looking at his face. *Unfortunately, I can't reprogram their core function. I've tried. The machines will conquer the biological part of you in the end. The only option is to get rid of them.*

Dread chilled her to the bones. *How am I supposed to get rid of them?*

They are sensitive to certain ionic frequencies. With the right kind of electromagnetic pulse, they become inert. Of all things, it felt like Doug gave her a wicked grin. *I believe your Denaidan friend may be able to help you with that.*

What are you talking about? Lisa's adrenaline was making her thoughts jumpy. *I can't even wake up right now, let alone find Qaiyaan, regain control of the ship, or defeat the rakwiji on board.*

I can't help you with the rakwiji, but I can reset your nanites for now and help you with the ship. With that, Doug grabbed hold of her nanites and twisted their programming at the same time he shattered the ship's lockouts. As she reeled from the backlash of power, his presence receded into the abyss. *Love you, Little Sis.*

Qaiyaan slapped the airlock button, barely waiting for the door to open before squeezing himself inside. Lisa had done it. This could only mean she was alive. *Lisa, you did it! I'm in!*

No answer. Was she unconscious? Mek had said it was dangerous for her to use her nanites. Possibly even deadly. He had to get to her, quickly.

Inside the airlock, the interior seal stood ajar. The bounty hunters had re-engaged gravity, but not life support, which probably meant they were suited up. Wouldn't they be surprised to discover the crew could resist vacuum? *Most of the crew.* The Denaidan ability to endure space wouldn't help Lisa if the bounty hunters forced open the door. He had to get life support up and running.

Depressing the button to close both doors, he slipped between the gleaming, angular machinery that filled Tovik's domain. The engineering control panel was near the ladder up to the main level. Where were the bounty hunters at this moment? It was too much to hope they'd come straight to engineering. They'd head for the control room, and Lisa'd said they carried pistols.

He looked around for a weapon, anything that might improve his chances against armed invaders. Next to the burn drive, Tovik's messy tool cabinet hung open, spanners and spare parts strewn across the decking. A battered pulse pistol lay among the scattered items.

Qaiyaan snatched it up and tucked it into his waistband. These bounty hunters were going to regret boarding his ship. He reinitiated life support, knowing the hiss of air through the ducts would take away the element of surprise.

Pistol ready, he poked his head from the trap door. The corridor was empty. From the direction of the med bay, a grunt of pain broke through the thin air. He pulled himself clear of the hatch and launched himself toward the open door. Inside, the floor was littered with broken medical equipment. Two rakwiji, their scales rippling with excitement, held Mek trapped in one corner. He stood bracing himself against the cabinet with both arms, his shirt slashed and darkened with turquoise blood. Tovik and Noatak both lay unconscious on their beds.

The smaller rakwiji slashed out with a knife, adding to the cuts on Mek's chest. Mek flinched but had nowhere to go. The larger bounty hunter, who held a pulse pistol aimed at the doctor's head, removed its helmet, revealing a flared crest of scales as it lifted its muzzle toward the hissing life support duct.

"Hey!" Qaiyaan shouted, taking aim at the larger rakwiji and pulling the trigger.

Nothing happened.

Both rakwiji bared gleaming razor teeth and the big one swiveled its gun toward Qaiyaan.

Qaiyaan pulled the useless trigger again then flung the weapon at his attackers before ducking back into the corridor. Plasma from the rakwiji's weapon impacted the corridor wall behind him, sending visible ripples of heat through the air. The smaller bounty hunter burst around the corner on the heels of the blast, still armed with the curved knife.

Typical rakwiji. They got off on playing with their prey. Qaiyaan obliged by stepping forward and ramming an ionically-powered fist into his attacker's scaled solar plexus. The surge of power through his already tired system threatened to buckle his knees, and his knuckles flared in pain against the creature's hard thorax. But the pressure sent the rakwiji flying halfway down the hall.

The bigger creature burst through the door and slammed into Qaiyaan, crashing him to the deck. Its cloyingly sweet yet sulfurous breath made Qaiyaan's eyes water.

Bringing up a knee, Qaiyaan wedged it between their bodies, using his ionic power to hurl this attacker off. He rolled toward the med bay, reaching for the bounty hunter's pulse pistol where it had fallen to the floor.

The big rakwiji lunged again, burying a necrotic claw into Qaiyaan's calf. Leg flaring in agony, Qaiyaan twisted, snarling at his attacker. Yanking its claw free, the bounty hunter opened its toothy mouth, its words a throaty growl. "I will peel that shiny copper skin from your body before you die."

Venom pulsed a fiery trail up Qaiyaan's leg. He had only minutes until it reached his heart. He had to kill his attacker now, before it finished him and moved on to his crew and Lisa. Both hearts pounding furiously, he grabbed a scalpel from the scattered implements on the floor. He jackknifed toward his attacker, slashing the blade at its throat.

The scalpel skittered ineffectually across the rakwiji's scaled hide.

The rakwiji laughed, tongue lolling between its spear-tipped grin. It opened its mouth wider and lunged as if to tear out Qaiyaan's throat.

Qaiyaan thrust the scalpel forward again, aiming for the creature's mouth. Humid breath encircled his hand and wrist, razor-sharp teeth grazing his skin. The rakwiji stiffened, trying to halt, but there was too much momentum behind its attack. With every ounce of ionic power he had left, Qaiyaan drove the blade upward through the rakwiji's palette and into its brain.

The beast collapsed, teeth digging into Qaiyaan's arm as it fell. From the doorway, the smaller rakwiji made a horrific screech as a pulse pistol blast cut the air above Qaiyaan's head. The creature turned and fled.

Twisting to free himself from the death throes of the big rakwiji, Qaiyaan spotted Mek holding both pulse pistols in trembling hands. The doctor set the weapons aside and turned to fumble in his medical supply cabinet.

Qaiyaan tried to rise to his feet, but the poison was taking hold of his muscle control. The skin showing through the tear in his pants was no longer copper, but a gnarled and lumpy web of black as the poison leached into his bloodstream. He flopped awkwardly against the deck. "I need to get to Lisa."

"We need to reverse the poison or you'll be dead within minutes. *Ellam Cua*, I know I have a vial of antidote here somewhere. Aha!" Mek turned, holding an inoculation gun and a handful of vials. "Hold on, captain. This'll take a minute to work."

Qaiyaan's tongue had grown too thick to speak. While Mek cut away his pants, Qaiyaan stared at the door where the alien had disappeared. *Lisa, can you hear me? They're coming!*

Lisa opened her eyes, her head pounding. The control panel still scrolled its diagnostics, all systems green. He'd done it! Thank God! *Doug are you still there?* No response. *Qaiyaan, can you hear me?* She received a garbled blast of pain instead of words. *Qaiyaan!*

Leaning forward to look at the camera images, she clutched the arms of the chair. A huge rakwiji had a claw buried in Qaiyaan's leg. "No!"

She lurched upright, but the chair's gravity restraints held her down. Fumbling with the buckles, she followed the struggle on the monitor. *Qaiyaan!* She wriggled loose and started for the door, then paused. A weapon. She needed a weapon. She scoured the small control room. How could these men call themselves pirates when they didn't even keep weapons in here?

Her gaze lit upon the small holocube of Noatak's family. It wouldn't be much of a threat as a missile, but the dozens of small beams it used to form the holo-image could be focused to create a low-level torch. *Better than nothing.* Muttering a quick apology to Noatak, she grabbed the cube and cracked open the casing. Weapon in hand, she cycled open the airlock door.

A rakwiji stood in the corridor clutching a curved knife.

It growled, spittle flying from its teeth and head crest flaring. Lisa swung her makeshift laser toward its face, squeezing the power cell. Her aim was off. The modified beam danced ineffectually across the rakwiji's shoulder.

A wide row of pointed teeth slowly appeared on its face. "The little human tries to poke me with a pin light? Do you think I am a Xeimir worm, afraid of the sun?"

Lisa's heart hammered. The rakwiji was so close, she could smell its sulfurous breath. The lasers might not be able to pierce its scaled hide, but that didn't mean her weapon was worthless. Taking aim again, she slashed the light across the bridge of the creature's muzzle, pointing it directly into its eyes.

The rakwiji dropped the knife, roaring and pressing both hands over its face. Unfortunately, it also remained blocking the doorway.

Praying the blindness lasted, Lisa crouched to retrieve the knife from beneath its feet.

The rakwiji slashed the air where she'd stood only moments before.

Blade in hand, Lisa squirmed backward, keeping the navigator seat between her and the yowling rakwiji. The blade would be useless against its scales, but it still felt better to be holding a weapon.

"You will be my final trophy." The rakwiji's eyes wept tears, and the entire room stank from its breath. "My mate and I will rut over your pain throughout eternity."

Lisa searched for a way out, but the rakwiji's bulk left no room to slip past. Sooner or later, its claws would find her. She shrank against the control panel, palm slick around the knife handle. The rakwiji took another shuffling step forward, still cursing, its legs wide as it sought her out.

Her gaze fell on the one place a rakwiji didn't have scales—its crotch. Dropping to her hands and knees, Lisa squeezed under the edge of the navigator's chair. She only had one chance. Once she let the creature know where she was, it would bury its claws into her. Pulling back her arm, she coiled every ounce of her strength.

The rakwiji stepped forward.

She drove the weapon into its genitals.

The knife sank to the hilt, sending hot blood pouring over Lisa's fingers. The rakwiji's expletives cut off mid-insult.

Yanking the knife free, Lisa somersaulted forward. She reached the door and chanced a look over her shoulder.

The bounty hunter was on its knees, clawed hands between its legs. A geyser of blood pulsed from between its fingers. "*Rrhuk'ni* carry me into the afterlife where I may rut in the blood of my enemies for all eternity."

Lisa curled her lips in disgust. "Have fun trying to enjoy your afterlife without any junk, you asshole."

She then fled toward the medical bay.

CHAPTER FIFTEEN

Qaiyaan opened his eyes, surrounded by the familiar walls of his cabin, to find Lisa gazing down at him.

Her cool hand brushed the hair from his forehead. "You're awake."

She was touching him. Lying next to him on his bunk, propped on one elbow, her body pressed along his. Which could only mean one thing; they were both dead, and this was *Ellam Cua's* final gift. He reached out to stroke her satin cheek. "I'm sorry."

"For what?"

"For letting us die. But I'm glad *Ellam Cua* has placed us together."

Lisa smiled and leaned forward to brush her lips against his. "We're not dead, silly."

Qaiyaan wrapped his hand around the back of her neck and drew her toward him again, craving her musky lilac scent. Her lips felt pliable and oh, so real. "I'm touching you," he murmured against her softness. "So we're either dead or this is a dream."

Her tongue flickered between his lips, teasing him. For long moments he was lost in the coaxing warmth of her mouth, the intimacy of her pillowy breasts against his side. His cock throbbed in response, but his leg still tingled from the rakwiji's venom. He wished the fatigue hadn't followed him into death. The afterlife was supposed to be free of pain and worry. Plus, there were several very naughty things he wanted to do to her. He traced his fingers along her shoulder blade, following the curve around her side and under her arm to cup her heavy breast. The nipple hardened beneath her shirt.

She moaned and slid one hand down his chest to rest upon his erection, and he realized he wore only his briefs. *Convenient.* He pumped his hips upward and groaned, the pressure of someone else's hand a sensation he'd not felt in over fifteen years.

Her fingers slipped inside his briefs and wrapped hotly around his shaft. "I dare say you are very much alive."

With a surge of motion, he flipped her onto her back so he could take over the lovemaking.

She sucked in a breath, her brows raised. He paused, realizing how rough he'd been. How *real*. This wasn't a dream. He twisted to look at his injured leg. The poison had left a dark spiderweb of broken capillaries up and down its surface, but whatever antidote Mek'd given him must've worked, because other than the residual ache, he felt fine. Alive. And very, very horny.

He returned his gaze to Lisa's, both hearts threatening to pour their way out of his chest. "How're we touching?"

"I found Doug." She grabbed his beard with both fists, her eyes dark with desire. "Don't stop what you're doing."

His thoughts spun, unable to keep up as he lowered himself to her mouth. Hope and lust surged through him. "He fixed your nanites?"

"Not exactly. He says I need to destroy them." She brought one leg up around his hip, then the other, squeezing with her heels until his cock ground against her. "He seems to think this might do it."

Despite the throbbing desire in his cock, Qaiyaan paused. "Whoa, slow down. Might?" He pushed up onto both hands to look down at her. "I thought you needed your nanites for us to be together."

"What I need is your cock inside me. Right now."

Her words alone were nearly enough to make him come. "*Ellam Cua*, woman! I need to know I won't kill you before we go any farther."

She sighed and eased the pressure of her heels. "Let me try this. It's faster."

Inside his head, a flurry of information appeared, as if she was reading him a book on fast forward. He experienced her joy and her sorrow while speaking to Doug, and understood the mystery of her nanites in ways he'd never imagined possible. She once again tugged his beard, trying to draw him toward her. "I have to destroy my nanites before they destroy me. And the only way to get rid of them is with an ionic pulse." Her lips twisted into a sassy smile. "Doug suggested yours."

He lowered himself to within kissing range. "Mine specifically?"

She pressed tiny kisses to his throat beneath the line of his beard, working her way toward his ear. "Yours."

Qaiyaan groaned. His cock was so hard, it was painful. Years of self-control warred inside him. "Are you sure you want to? What if…"

"Mek's standing by. And yes. I want to feel you inside me." Her breathy voice against his ear sent a shiver to his toes.

Turning his head, he captured her lips in a kiss. The sweet pressure of her tongue in his mouth was pure bliss. Slowly, savoring every moment, he kissed her, cupping her cheek with one hand. His other hand sought a breast, teasing the nipple into a rigid peak. The intimacy of her body close to his was something he'd never thought possible, but even stronger was the soft and gentle pressure of her thoughts brushing against his. Her lust for him rivaled his. He reached for the latch on her waistband, wanting to feel her. To sink his fingers into her dusky curls. To feel her slick opening part for him.

She wriggled, lifting her hips to help him shimmy her legs free of her clothing. Her hands roamed his torso, as desperate for him as he was for her. Her gasping breaths fanned his desire.

Pants removed, he pulled back, looking down at her body. He'd never seen anything more beautiful. Charcoal depths of her eyes filled with lust, she let her legs fall open to expose her soft, wet entrance and held her hands toward him, seeking to draw him near.

He swallowed, offering one last attempt at control. "I won't be able to stop if we go any farther."

She scooted her bottom closer to him, spreading her thighs even wider, and lifted herself so her backside rested against his thighs. "Shut up and fuck me."

Groaning, he dragged her hips toward him until the head of his cock grazed her slitted heat. The slick folds caressed his length with delicious, slippery promise. She quivered, fingertips digging into his forearms as she wrapped her legs around his hips.

Qaiyaan shuddered, the head of his cock glistening with pre-come. If he wasn't careful, he might fulfill Tovik's prediction and finish before he'd even started. He ground his teeth, holding back while she wriggled, part of him still resisting this final commitment. Then she reached down, grabbing his shaft and settling the head against the center of her opening. Without conscious thought, his hips surged forward.

Her heat enveloped him in sheer bliss.

"*Ellam Cua*," he breathed, eyes rolling back in his head. His hands dug into her hips, holding her steady. "Don't move."

"I can't help it!" She threw her head back, heels digging hard into his backside, driving him deeper than he thought possible. Her core pulsed around him, on the edge of orgasm. She whimpered and licked her lips, her pink tongue an invitation. He fell forward to kiss her again. Tangling his tongue with hers, he thrust forward, crushing her body beneath his. She accepted every thrust, pumping her legs in time to his rhythm. Deeper, harder, faster.

A moan rose from her lips, a sound that resonated in his chest as if she were the one with ionic power rather than the other way around. Her voice grew higher, and he moved faster, knowing she was almost at her peak. The base of his spine tingled with electric desire, balls tightening with the need for release. *No, not yet, hold on a little longer...*

She grabbed his beard, her back arching. "Qaiyaan!" Her pussy convulsed around him and her entire body quaked with her release.

His balls exploded, his vision bursting into a million stars...

When he came to his senses, he lay on top of her, panting. Horrified, he pulled back, clumsy-drunk from his orgasm. He never remembered coming so hard in his life. He searched her face. Cheeks flushed and eyes closed, she had a slight smile on her lips. Sending out a small ionic nudge, he detected her heartbeat, steady and quick. Her body was alive, then, but what about her mind?

He spoke her name in a reverent hush. "Lisa?"

She turned her head slightly without opening her eyes. "Mmm?"

He let out his breath in a whoosh and lowered himself until his forehead touched hers. This was a miracle he'd never expected. A gift he didn't deserve. "You survived."

"Did I? I'm not so sure." She wrapped both arms around his chest and dug her heels into his backside. "I think we need to try again."

"Your nanites?"

Only a momentary pause, then her luscious mouth spread into a grin. "Gone."

Qaiyaan tilted his head to meet her lips, his heart soaring. His cock had fifteen years of celibacy to make up for.

Lisa sat at the galley table, trying to pay attention to the crew's conversation about the cartel ship now sitting in their hold, but even with Qaiyaan seated at the opposite side of the table, she couldn't keep from touching him. She slid one bare foot up the inside of his leg until his hand caught it near his crotch.

His face remained impassive, but he pressed the ball of her foot against his bulging erection while he spoke. "How much can we get for it? We need to fix our hull." His gaze met hers, lust simmering beneath the surface. "We have precious cargo aboard."

Lisa felt every eye in the galley fall on her. She flushed, still uncomfortable with their awe. "You guys need to stop doing that. I'm just another member of the crew."

"A loud member." Noatak smirked at her.

The heat in her face intensified, and she tried to draw her foot back, but Qaiyaan held firm, massaging her arch with one thumb. His cheek twitched with mirth. The bastard was enjoying her embarrassment. She muttered under her breath. "Damned thin-walled ship."

Tovik nodded, his copper face flushed with iridescent blue-green. "Noatak, I'd be happy to put up a hammock for you in engineering. The engines help buffer the... noise."

Now Lisa's face felt like it was about to burst into flames. She'd never been prudish about her sex life, but she'd also never had a group of men so focused on it. These guys needed women of their own. She turned to Mek. "How are the nanites doing?"

The mood in the room sobered. The physical changes the nanites had made to her body allowed her to be with Qaiyaan, but now her nanites were gone. She was no longer a source for additional samples. With only a few remaining vials in existence from her previous tests, the doctor worried there weren't enough to continue his testing, let alone enough to create new, compatible mates.

Mek shook his head, his gaze sliding away from hers. "I've not been successful in culturing more of them. They need a host."

Tovik leaned forward. "So we go find some hosts."

Noatak thrust a restraining palm toward the younger man. "Slow down, Tovik. You don't want to end up with just any random woman."

"There could also be side effects to the nanites themselves." Mek scratched at one stubbled cheek. "I just don't know enough, and we have a limited supply for testing."

Lisa sat up straighter, this time successfully pulling her foot free of Qaiyaan's grasp. "Doug has nanites." The only thing that had remotely intruded on her new infatuation with Qaiyaan was the knowledge that her brother was alive and in Syndicorp hands. "When we free him, we'll have all the samples you need."

"I thought he didn't tell you where he was?" Noatak said.

"I can still hack into the darkweb, even without my nanites. That's where I'll pick up a trail to the Syndicorp lab, I just know it. I only need access to a boosted console."

"I can boost our array pretty easily," Tovik offered. "I already stripped a bunch of the comm webbing off the cartel ship."

Qaiyaan flinched. "You did what?"

Tovik drew his shoulders up to his ears and grimaced. "And I accidentally fried the control hydraulics when I tried to incorporate the secondary stage burners into our forward drive."

Noatak dropped his chin and shook his head. "At least you didn't blow the *Hardship's* systems." Sighing, he stood. "Well, let's get Lisa set up on a console."

"Cool your jets, everyone." Qaiyaan rose. "The darkweb is a sketchy place. I don't want to put Lisa in any more danger. You know how important she is to me."

Noatak turned. "She's important to us all, *Iluq*. And she's the only one with a plan at the moment."

Lisa stood and wrapped her arms around Qaiyaan's solid waist. "I'll be sitting at a console. No nanites involved. I'll be fine."

He enveloped her in his amber-scented embrace, shaking his head. "We can't go anywhere until we get our hull fixed."

"You're just making excuses." Lisa tilted her head to look up into his face. "There's no reason I can't start looking into the darkweb while you do the hull repairs."

"Last time I went outside to look at the hull we almost all died."

"So you're just going to not look at it ever again? That's no solution."

Tovik threw both hands into the air. "Listen! That's what I was trying to tell you guys. The hull's all good."

"How?" Qaiyaan asked.

"I sort of borrowed most of the plating off that cartel ship."

The other three men groaned in unison. Noatak slumped against the doorjamb. "Is there anything left of that ship to sell?"

"The hull needed fixing." Tovik shrugged and looked sideways at Lisa with a wink. "And I needed to go outside for some peace and quiet."

Lisa grinned back at him, pressing her cheek against Qaiyaan's solid chest. Tovik was feeling more and more like a little brother by the moment. Doug was going to get a real kick out of him.

"There're some pretty good parts left to sell," Tovik continued, and began rattling off flux modulators and other parts, ticking each item off on his fingers. "Although I want to save the fuel matrixes for a fixed acceleration project I've been working on."

Qaiyaan's voice was low and gruff, but Lisa could sense amusement behind his words. "Tovik, one of these days we're going to have to start charging you for your little science experiments."

"My experiments have paid for themselves almost every time." Tovik crossed his arms and scowled. "I get no appreciation around here."

Lisa released Qaiyaan, sliding a hand down his arm to entwine her fingers with his. "Then I guess we'll start looking for Doug?"

Qaiyaan's fingers tightened around hers. "Let's go kick some Syndicorp ass."

Dear Reader,

Ready to find mates for more sexy Denaidan pirates? Up next is Captain Kashatok!

She's disguised as a boy
on a ship full of sex-crazed aliens...
What could possibly go wrong?

Tap the cover to get Ransomed by Kashatok now, or keep reading for an excerpt!

XOXO

Tamsin

P.S. I'd like to offer you a free prequel story for joining my VIP Club newsletter. Visit Denaida-daru and meet

Kashatok's first love in this exclusive VIP Club short story. JOIN HERE > https://BookHip.com/LJJTWF

Ransomed by Kashatok
Excerpt

Facing the cantina's dirty restroom mirror, Joy gripped a hunk of her curly brown hair in one hand and scissors in the other. Behind her, a wall-length screen flickered with an ad for inter-alien contraceptive products, haloing her with eerie green light. *Just do it*, she thought. *Hair grows back, no big deal.* Except that her mother, a Syndicorp Communications CEO, already liked to goad her about her fashion sense, saying it was a good thing Joy was smart, because she'd never get by on her looks. Yet even being smart wasn't good enough, not unless Joy used it to climb the corporate ladder.

When Joy signed on as a reporter with RealTime news, her mother'd almost disowned her. How was she going to react when she found out Joy was doing an undercover exposé? *At least I'm not disguising myself as a prostitute.* Not that her producer at RealTime hadn't hinted at how sensational *that* would be. But Joy had tools other than her tits to secure this story. Being tall for a woman, she'd decided to go the complete opposite direction with her disguise. Her canvas cargo pants and mechanic shirt were boxy and genderless, and she'd even gone so far as to wrap her breasts to mask her curves. She just needed the finishing touch.

Taking a deep breath, she squeezed the scissors. Her long tresses fell away with an oddly satisfying sensation. A lopsided reflection stared back at her with startled gray eyes. "No going back now," she muttered.

Her square jaw wasn't quite manly, but she was plain enough that with the right attitude, she could pass for a boy. And she'd already proven she had attitude doing a year of volunteer work for Syndicorp's emergency services division in their fleet mechanic shop. Joy'd loved the hands-on problem-solving and the smell of hydraulic fluid and hot metal until Mother learned she wasn't handing out cookies and pulled her.

Satisfied with her hair, Joy pulled mascara out of her purse and dabbed it beneath her nails, rubbing it into her skin for good measure. No one trusted a mechanic with clean hands. When she was satisfied, she once again looked into the mirror, winking her left eye to engage her cybernetic camera. A recording of her reflection would make a decent, gritty opening scene for the exposé. One benefit of having a Communications CEO for a mother was that Joy had access to technology other newbie reporters would die for.

"I'm at the edge of unclassified space, looking for information about pirate activity. These ruthless men and women have been plaguing the shipping lanes since Syndicorp sent its first colonization envoys outside the Alleigh system." Joy spoke in a husky, conspiratorial tone, glancing over her shoulder at the restroom door. The chances of someone entering were slim to none with the hotel door grav-loc she'd placed against the door stop, but her pulse beat loudly in her ears even so. "Stay tuned as I go undercover into the swashbuckling world of black market trading and deep-space piracy —bleh."

Sighing, she stopped the camera. She sounded like a game show host. Everything about this broadcast had to be perfect. Serious. Anchor-worthy.

She tried again. "My informant just sent word there's a notorious pirate in this very bar. I'm going to try to join his crew. For the next few weeks, I'll be broadcasting the RealTime stories of these men."

The door rattled. Joy quickly cached the recordings on her polycom to edit later and removed the grav-loc, brushing past the annoyed Saluqan woman outside. "Watch it. Door sticks," Joy mumbled and dove into the crowded cantina. She had a pirate captain to find.

Captain Kashatok pried Jhikik's tail from around the bottle of Kantarellian rum and poured himself another tall serving. On board ship, he often drank straight from the bottle. For the purpose of interviewing new crew members, he was attempting to look civilized. He had enough rough edges on his crew, and attracting yet another discipline problem was not in his plan today.

The little netorpok chittered at him in reprimand and climbed up his arm to sit on his shoulder, his lavender fur tickling Kashatok's ear. Jhikik had come into his possession as a pup, and, much like a real child, liked to nag him about his vice. "Keep it down."

Too late. A woman who'd been perched on a stool at the bar was heading in his direction, her sizable cleavage jiggling above the low neckline of her tight blouse with every step. Happened every time. First, she'd fawn over the netorpok, then turn her attention to the broad-shouldered owner. Women loved a man with a pet. And Jhikik loved the attention.

"There's a reason I never leave the ship," Kashatok muttered, glowering at the woman. Female company was never on his agenda and never would be.

Thankfully, the oncoming woman took the hint and veered toward the restrooms. As the cantina's band started up a new set, Kashatok rose from his chair and scanned the dark interior of the cantina for his first mate's shaggy head. Aleknagik was supposed to be escorting prospective shuttle mechanics to the table for interviews. Across the dimly lit floor, cantina patrons parted like an outgoing tide around the tall, copper-skinned Denaidan. *About time he found someone.* Settling back into his chair, Kashatok downed the rest of the rum in his glass. Aleknagik pulled up to the table and stopped.

Kashatok scanned the conspicuously empty space around to the big man. "Well?"

Aleknagik shook his head. "Word's gotten around about what happened to our last mechanic."

The muscle in Kashatok's jaw tightened. "And?"

"No one's exactly excited to be the next one tossed out the airlock."

"I have one hard rule. No women aboard my ship." Not only that, but what the mechanic had been doing to that poor female deserved retribution.

Sliding out a chair, Aleknagik sat heavily, the reek of cirripi weed wafting off him. He leaned forward, both elbows on the table. "Listen, I understand why you made that rule. But with those nanites Captain Qaiyaan's been talking about, we might be able to change that. Plus your non-Denaidan crew members might appreciate some leeway."

Kashatok gritted his teeth. The *Kinship*'s core crew of Denaidans were unable to enjoy the pleasures of women, and Kashatok's rule had never made much of a difference to them. Until the nanites. Once again, Syndicorp had planted a seed of hope within the Denaidans. No, not a seed. A spore. A *virus*. A Syndicorp engineered virus. And it was fucking with his ship. "My ship—my rules. If someone's not okay with that, they can get the fuck off."

His first mate frowned but kept silent, his eyes full of questions and distrust.

Grabbing the rum, Kashatok took a long pull of the burning liquid. There'd never be a woman for him, anyway, nanites or not. He couldn't be trusted, not after

Aiyana... He took another swallow. His past was none of Aleknagik's business.

An olive-skinned human appeared just past Aleknagik's shoulder, wide gray eyes darting between the back of the first mate's head and Kashatok. The moment their eyes met, Kashatok felt a jolt, a desire to protect that was at odds with the hard-assed captain he tried to be. The kid reminded him of his own first insecure days off-planet, seeking jobs in seedy cantinas just like this one. The visitor moved up beside the first mate, both hands shoved deep in the front pockets of his baggy cargo pants. "You're looking for a shuttle mechanic?"

Aleknagik twisted in his seat, eyes nearly level with their visitor's. "You know one?"

The young man stretched a hand forward. "Name's Joey."

"You?" Aleknagik laughed.

Jhikik leaped from Kashatok's shoulder onto the tabletop. Kashatok snatched hold of the tip of the creature's tail, drawing him up short. Not everyone appreciated the creature's curiosity.

Turning to Kashatok, Aleknagik jerked a thumb toward Joey, eyes dancing with mirth. "What do you say,

Captain? Think this *qumli* could hold his own among our crew?"

The kid was barely old enough to leave his mother's teat, let alone stand up to a rowdy crew. Kashatok sent out a tightly-controlled ionic pulse. Alcohol dulled his sensitivity, but he could still assess the kid's heartbeat, breathing, and skin temperature. Joey was nervous, for sure. But his hands were dirty, and the look in his eye was hungry. Would it hurt to let him have his say? Kashatok pushed the rum bottle forward without accepting the handshake. "Have a seat."

Dropping his hand, Joey pulled out a chair and sat. He didn't touch the rum. They locked gazes and Kashatok had to hand it to him, the kid didn't look away. "You don't seem old enough to be a mechanic."

Joey shrugged one shoulder. "Only been at it a year, but I'm a fast learner."

Kashatok retrieved the bottle and tilted back for a long swallow. May as well let the kid see the real him. "You familiar with the CrossX Spacer Elite?"

"Sure." Joey tilted his head and squinted his eyes in thought. "I helped with a thruster rebuild. And adjusted the flux coil on one of the newer models."

"Huh," said Aleknagik, nodding. "Where're you from?"

Joey scowled. "Why's that matter?"

Aleknagik dropped his bearded chin to glower back. Jhikik crept forward, eyes on the stranger.

"What?" Joey crossed his arms. "Pirates don't have pasts. Or they shouldn't."

Kashatok repressed a smile. This kid might just be capable of holding his own after all. He stroked his fingertips along Jhikik's long tail until the little creature spun and batted at his hand. "You heard about our last mechanic?"

The young man's left eye twitched. "Tell me."

"Space-locked." Kashatok paused a moment. Joey's heart beat so rapidly, Kashatok barely had to engage his ionic senses to feel it.

"By you?"

Kashatok nodded slowly, keeping eye contact. "There's only one unbreakable rule on the *Kinship*. You can't bring women on board. Think you can handle that?"

Joey took a long breath and let it out slowly. "That's all? Sounds easy. What's my cut?"

"Ha!" Aleknagik clapped the young man on the shoulder, rocking him forward. "I like him!"

Joey kept his gaze on the captain.

For some reason, Kashatok hadn't expected the mercenary question, probably because the kid had seemed more interested in the adventure than the money. "Probation gets you one share. Things work out after the first score or two, we'll talk more."

Nodding, Joey once again thrust out his hand. "Deal."

This time, Kashatok took it. The palm was softer than he'd expected, but maybe that was just a human thing. "We're parked in slip A21P. I'll be pulling out as soon as we're restocked, so I suggest you get your ass aboard sooner rather than later."

"Aye aye, captain."

Alek laughed again. "We don't say that, human."

Joey licked his lips, and Kashatok found the move oddly disturbing. "Sorry," said the kid. "I do call you captain though, right?"

"I don't care what you call me, as long as you do your job." Kashatok rose, grabbing the rum bottle and holding out an arm for Jhikik. The netorpok gave Joey a longing look, then skittered up to rest on Kashatok's shoulder.

As Kashatok turned to leave, Joey called out, "I'll keep your shuttle in top shape."

Kashatok kept moving. Behind him, he heard Alek giving advice. "Young man like you's got urges. Long as you take care of them off-ship, you'll be fine. Oh, and stay away from the captain's rum."

Stopping at the crowded bar, Kashatok ordered one last bottle to go.

Get Ransomed by Kashatok and keep reading now!

Glossary

- *Anaq* - Shit
- **Attahat wheel** - A form of gambling using a random wheel much like roulette
- **Burn** - The means by which ships travel long distances quickly using ionic frequencies to bend space
- **Cartel** - Organized crime ring
- **Cochlear implant** - A cybernetic device that transmits communications via vibrations directly against the bones of the ear
- **Denaida-daru** - The Denaidan homeworld, destroyed by Syndicorp. Also called planet K-4H10
- *Ellam Cua* - The Denaidan deity
- **Enayshuan** - A human-like species with prominent eye ridges, known for their metallic

body powder. Often associated with the sex trade

- **Finofan** - Aliens with iguana-like frills around their ears and slitted eyes. They like hot and humid atmosphere
- **Garan'uk** - A methane breathing alien species
- *Iluq* - Brother
- **Ionic power or shield** - A Denaidan ability to affect matter and gravity
- **Kwirn** - A form of gambling using 3-D tables and pieces
- **Nav-grav seats** - Used to keep humanoids comfortable during ship burn
- **Netorpok** - An exotic pet banned on most worlds
- **Parsec** - A measurement of distance (3.2 light years)
- **Posungi** - An egg-laying alien with an orange tentacled face
- *Qumli* - Asshole
- **Rakwiji** - Scaled aliens with a poisonous claw, who hunt in pairs and require torture as part of their mating ritual. Often hired by the cartel as bounty hunters
- **Sizantha pods** - Used to make tea
- **Syndicorp** - A mega-corporation that runs a huge section of the galaxy

- **The Termination** - Syndicorp's destruction of Denaida-daru
- *Ucuk* - Dick
- *Uminaq* - Dammit
- **Unclassified space** - Areas of the galaxy not ruled by Syndicorp
- **Xeimir worm** - A glossy-skinned alien that breathes through its skin and is ultra-sensitive to light
- **Yanipa-nimayu** - A six-legged alien often found performing manual labor

Also by Tamsin Ley

Galactic Pirate Brides series

Galactic Pirate Brides Box Set (Includes first 3 books)

Rescued by Qaiyaan

Ransomed by Kashatok

Claimed by Noatak

Taken by the Cyborg

Mates for Monsters

Mer-Lovers Collector's Edition (Includes first 3 books)

The Merman's Kiss

The Merman's Quest

A Mermaid's Heart

The Centaur's Bride

The Djinn's Desire

Khargals of Duras

Sticks and Stones

Alaska Alphas

Alpha Origins

Untamed Instinct

Bewitched Shifter

Midnight Heat

Wild Child

Kirenai Fated Mates (Intergalactic Dating Agency)

Kirenai Fated Mates Boxset (Includes first 3 books)

Arazhi

Zhiruto

Iroth

POST-APOCALYPTIC SCIENCE FICTION WRITTEN AS TAM LINSEY

Botanicaust

The Reaping Room

Doomseeds

Amarantox

ABOUT THE AUTHOR

Once upon a time I thought I wanted to be a biomedical engineer, but experimenting on lab rats doesn't always lead to happy endings. Now I blend my nerdy infatuation of science with character-driven romance and guaranteed happily-ever-afters. My monsters always find their mates, with feisty heroines, tortured heroes, and all the steamy trouble they can handle. I promise my stories will never leave you hanging (although you may still crave more!)

When I'm not writing, I'll be in the garden or the kitchen, exploring Alaska with my husband, or preparing for the zombie apocalypse.

Interested in more about me? Join my VIP Club and get free books, notices, and other cool stuff!

www.tamsinley.com

bookbub.com/authors/tamsin-ley

goodreads.com/TamsinLey

facebook.com/TamsinLey

amazon.com/author/tamsin

Made in the USA
Coppell, TX
03 January 2024

27184554R00118